KU-021-555

more of
Gary Lineker's
Favourite Football Stories

Having been one of the world's most acclaimed football players, Gary Lineker has now become a highly successful television personality. He is presenter of the BBC TV magazine programme *Football Focus*, and a team captain in the hugely popular quiz show *They Think It's All Over*. He also researched and presented the major eight-part BBC series *Gary Lineker's Golden Boots*, in which he travelled through Europe and South America to interview some of the greatest goal-scorers of all time.

Gary Lineker's extraordinary footballing career took him from Leicester City to Everton, Barcelona, Tottenham Hotspur and Japan's Nagoya Grampus 8. He captained the England team from 1990 to 1992, and he is England's second highest goal-scorer, with one goal less than Sir Bobby Charlton.

Among many other commendations he received the Golden Boot Award for the top scorer of the 1986 World Cup, and was honoured with the OBE in 1992.

Also available

Gary Lineker's Favourite Football Stories

more of

GARY LINEKER'S

FAVOURITE FOOTBALL STORIES

MACMILLAN CHILDREN'S BOOKS

First published 1998 by Macmillan Children's Books

This edition published 1999 by Macmillan Children's Books
a division of Macmillan Publishers Limited
25 Eccleston Place, London SW1W 9NF
and Basingstoke

Associated companies throughout the world

ISBN 0 330 37075 8

This collection copyright © Macmillan Children's Books 1998
'Hat-Trick Hero' © Celia Warren 1998; 'Fixer' © Anthony Masters 1998; 'A Dog Called
Lineker' © Eric Johns 1998; 'Jessica's Brother' © Gus Grenfell 1998; 'The Boffin Bounces
Back' © David Harmer 1998; 'The Twitcher' © Redvers Brandling 1998; 'Much Ado About
Nothing' © Mick Gowar 1998; 'Strikers and Keepers' © John Goodwin 1998; 'Lyon Heart'
© Ann Ruffell 1998; 'Stickers' © Dave Ward 1998; 'Gary's Goal' © Alan Durant 1998;
'Gruesome Gran and the Broken Promise' © Trevor Millum 1998; 'Striking Out' © Pat
Leighton 1998; 'He's the Man!' © David Clayton 1998

The publishers would also like to thank Anthony Buckeridge for permission to include
'Jennings Uses His Head' from *Jennings Goes to School*, first published by Macmillan
Children's Books in 1996 and copyright © Anthony Buckeridge 1950, 1985, 1988, 1996

All rights reserved. No part of this publication may be reproduced,
stored in or introduced into a retrieval system, or transmitted,
in any form, or by any means (electronic, mechanical, photocopying,
recording or otherwise) without the prior written permission of the publisher.
Any person who does any unauthorized act in relation to
this publication may be liable to criminal prosecution
and civil claims for damages.

1 3 5 7 9 8 6 4 2

A CIP catalogue record for this book is available from
the British Library.

Phototypeset by Intype London Ltd
Printed and bound in Great Britain by Mackays of Chatham plc, Kent

This book is sold subject to the condition that it shall not,
by way of trade or otherwise, be lent, re-sold, hired out,
or otherwise circulated without the publisher's prior consent
in any form of binding or cover other than that in which
it is published and without a similar condition including this
condition being imposed on the subsequent purchaser.

CONTENTS

Welcome back, football fans!

I'm delighted you are able to join me for my second collection of sensational soccer stories, which I hope you'll agree is every bit as enthralling as the first. If you're a football fanatic, here's everything you could possibly need for hours and hours of first-rate footy fun!

Once again, here is a bumper bundle of action-packed stories that burst with excitement and drama, and which capture all the penalties and the pride, the friendships and the rivalries, the glory and the pain of the world's most amazing sport.

I hope you will really enjoy the book – and enjoy playing your own football too. As someone has said, football isn't a matter of life and death. It's *far* more important!

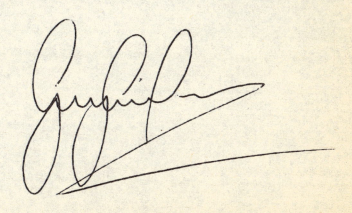

Hat-Trick Hero

Celia Warren

One minute Josh had been fast asleep. The next he was wide awake. He didn't know what had woken him. By the faint light of his bedside lamp, his eyes struggled to focus on his alarm clock. It was one o'clock in the morning.

Out of the corner of his eye, Josh saw a movement. His football was rolling slowly but deliberately across the carpet towards him, just as if someone had given it a gentle kick. It came to a standstill beside his bed.

Josh switched on the main light. He reached down for the ball. It felt warm, as if it had been left lying in the grass on a summer's day. Of course, he had left it in the corner by the radiator as he did every night. But what had made the ball roll by itself like that? Josh shivered and snuggled down under his quilt away from the cold night air. He left the light on while he went back to sleep.

'Morning, Joshua,' said his mother, six hours later, as she opened his curtains.

Sunshine flooded into Josh's bedroom. Good. It was going to be fine for the match. It was the first time Josh had been chosen for the school team and he wanted the day to be perfect. Now all he had to do was get through the grind of a morning's schoolwork and keep his excitement under control.

Josh rubbed his eyes and jumped out of bed. Automatically, he picked up his football and gave it a fond stroke, just like his sister, Alice, would give her guinea pig. It was not until he put the ball on his unmade bed that he remembered waking in the night. But surely he had just picked up the ball from beside the radiator, not from by the bed where it had rolled in the night? How odd!

'Mum must've put it back,' Josh said to himself, and thought no more about it.

As Josh's mother dropped him off at the school gate, she wished him luck.

'I'm sorry I shan't be able to watch you, Joshua,' she said. 'I'm afraid I just can't get away from work in time.'

Josh dodged out of the car before she could kiss him. Mum could be so embarrassing at times; like when she called him by his full name, Joshua.

'We're going to win tonight,' he told Alice, as they walked into the playground.

'I'm sure you will,' said Alice. 'I wish I could watch,' she added, 'but if I miss the auditions this afternoon I won't get a part in the panto.' Alice, like their mother, was keen on drama. Somehow Mum always managed to come and see Alice when she was acting. Josh wished he had a dad to come and cheer him on – but it was no good wishing.

'Your dad was never interested in football,' his mother had told him often enough, 'but *his* dad – your grandad – played all the time. He'd have been very proud of his grandson.'

Josh had never known his grandfather. Grandad Jim

2

had died before Josh was born, and Josh's dad had taken himself off to live and work in America when Josh was only a baby. He couldn't remember him at all.

The whistle blew. For a brief moment Josh thought he heard a crowd cheer and clap. It was as if someone had rapidly switched a radio on and then off again in the middle of a live broadcast of a football match. Josh shook his head. It was only a teacher, blowing the whistle in the playground. It was time to go into school.

The Head, Mr Henry, asked the team to stay behind after assembly. He reminded them of their responsibilities as hosts at that afternoon's home match. They must make the St Luke's team welcome. They must show good sportsmanship – it was the playing not the winning that counted . . .

Mr Henry's voice droned on. Josh's mind wandered. From the cloakroom the squeaky sound of a recorder drifted through to the hall. Someone was playing the theme tune to TV's *Match of the Day.*

Mr Henry's closing words jolted Josh back from his daydream.

'Now, some exciting news,' he said. 'There is to be a special feature about the school in the *Echo* this week. A photographer will be taking pictures of the match this afternoon, and I'm looking forward to seeing some exciting shots of you all in action. So now, heads down in the classroom and save your football thoughts for later. Off you go.'

As Josh turned to leave the hall, he felt a hand on his shoulder. It was Mr Henry.

'Your first inter-school match, isn't it?' he asked.

'Yes, sir,' nodded Josh.

'Good luck then, Jim,' smiled Mr Henry and marched off to his office before Josh could correct him.

'Oh well,' shrugged Josh. 'Jim's better than Joshua, I suppose.'

Time never goes so slowly as when you're waiting for something. The first half of the morning seemed endless. Break, when it finally came, was spent discussing tactics. Back in the classroom the morning dragged on and on.

Eventually lunchtime came. Josh was the first to get changed. Proudly, he ran with his friends on to the field to meet the St Luke's team. But even as they set off for a warm-up run around the field, the air was changing. It took on a sudden chill. Mist was beginning to rise from the nearby canal and drift across the school field. The games teacher from St Luke's and their own Mr Briggs had their heads together. Soon they blew the whistle and beckoned everyone over.

'This mist is already beginning to thicken,' said Mr Briggs. 'It's going to be difficult to see each other soon, never mind the goalposts.'

Josh and his mates grimaced. They knew how quickly these November mists turned to fog. Games often got cancelled at this time of year. Josh crossed his fingers.

'So we've agreed to shorten the game to thirty minutes each end, and we're starting now . . .'

St Luke's won the toss and chose the goal nearer the canal.

They're not stupid, thought Josh, as he looked at the clearly visible goal his team had to defend, compared with St Luke's goal, where the mist was already swirling around the net. On the other hand, they had the advantage of a slight slope.

The match began.

It was one of those games where the action is instant. Within seconds of St Luke's kick-off, Josh's team captain, Rob, had claimed control of the ball. Rob chipped it to Kev who headed it to Josh as they advanced down the field. Josh fed the ball through St Luke's line of defence but met stronger resistance from their goalkeeper. Back up the field went the ball. As Josh turned to pursue it, he realized just how quickly the mist was spreading. Already their own goal was almost hidden. St Luke's would have to work harder now.

Voices cut through the swirling fog, distorted in the damp air. Figures were growing harder to see as the mist spread patchily across the pitch. Josh could just make out that it was Kev who had succeeded in grabbing the ball back from St Luke's. As Josh shouted to Kev his voice sounded strange and detached, but Kev responded and the ball was Josh's.

He grabbed his chance. He plunged through the mist, weaving his way up the right wing, until he knew he had to pass the ball. Only one player was visible. Josh struck out and landed the ball in front of his team-mate's boot. A superb strike saw the ball fly home, past the goalkeeper's head, into the roof of the net.

As they ran back to the centre, Kev clapped Josh on the back. 'Brilliant shot,' he cried.

'That was some goal,' added Rob, their captain.

'It wasn't mine,' said Josh, breathlessly. 'I passed it to . . .'

Who was it? In the mist Josh hadn't been sure. It was a boy his own size. It might have been Andy. Josh gasped in the cold air and felt it as hard as glass in his lungs. He couldn't finish his sentence before everyone was in position and the ball was back in play.

St Luke's rallied and, having created an opening, they kept hold of the ball in a relentless attack. Twice Rob broke through their ranks only to have the ball taken back by a strong advance from St Luke's.

Now it was Josh's chance to tackle. He hurled himself forward. His boot connected with the ball but only briefly, and again the ball was disappearing towards its target. Now Andy tried to intervene, but the ball shot in the air off the end of a big St Luke's boot and slotted into their goal, scoring an equalizer.

'We're going to change ends now,' came Mr Briggs' voice. 'This mist is getting too thick too quickly.'

Josh glanced at his watch. They were only twenty minutes into the game. One–all, and only twenty minutes to go! He hated drawing. Josh's hands clutched his mud-encrusted knees. He tucked his head down. His boot lace was undone but he couldn't bend to tie it. He concentrated on his breath as it spread in a murky cloud to mix with the mist. In this half they would be playing upfield, but now both nets were lost in the mist. Josh took a painfully deep breath and watched Rob take the kick.

Motivated by their equalizer, St Luke's quickly took control. The ball switched from left to right, sometimes visible, sometimes obscured in the fog. All the players became an indistinguishable grey. Josh threw himself at the ball as a St Luke's striker flicked it right into his path. He shot it straight between the legs of the flailing opposition. Rob took it upfield and passed to Andy, who headed it straight back to Josh.

Josh kept moving, dragging the defence all over the place. He ran forward with the ball, skidded on the wet grass and recovered. His marker's boot shot towards the ball but, even as Josh swerved out of the tackle, the other boy lost his balance and landed with a squelch on the churned-up sludge.

A shout went up from the sidelines. *Yes, Yes, Yes!*

Josh felt the beads of sweat on his forehead. He could barely see the goal, but he fired. The goalkeeper was on it in an instant, palming it out of the goal mouth but, before he could follow up, Josh saw a boot, its lace flapping like his own, strike from a narrow angle. The ball flicked easily into the back of the St Luke's net.

'Goal!'

'Two—one!'

'Two scores, Josh!' cried Rob. 'Go for your hat-trick.'

'Well played, Josh.'

Even Mr Briggs was congratulating him now, as they ran back down the field.

'It wasn't me,' said Josh, but his voice was muffled in the mist and now the ball was back in play. He hadn't time to talk.

The second goal was a blow to St Luke's, but they were not dispirited for long. They quickly took the ball and kept hold of it. Their tallest, fastest striker pushed the ball towards the nearly invisible net. Emerging suddenly through the mist the shot took the lurking goalkeeper by surprise, but his quick reaction, a full-length dive, saved it. Brushing the hair from his eyes with the back of a muddy hand, he threw the ball

7

to Andy who dodged his marker with expertise, driving the ball over to Kev.

'Josh!' screamed Kev like a banshee in the fog, as he headed it over to his friend.

'This one's mine,' Josh responded and lashed out.

The ball spun through the air and bounced off the goalpost, momentarily disappearing in the mist, before it reappeared. Josh watched as, again, it was booted through the air and into the St Luke's goal. There was a flash from the sidelines, where the photographer from the *Echo* was trying to catch the scene despite the fog, and then the final whistle blew.

Only the cheer from his team confirmed to Josh that the ball had landed a third goal. Josh didn't see it. He kept his eye fixed on that one spot; the position of the player who had scored. He ran forward, searching for the invisible player. Who was it who was scoring all these goals?

Already Josh's friends were pressing round him with congratulations and cries of 'Hat-trick!' He shrugged them off, looking around him. Was it a St Luke's player who had a taste for scoring own-goals? he wondered, doubtfully.

'You mustn't be so modest,' Mr Briggs told him as they set off for the changing rooms. 'Visibility was poor to say the least, but nothing deterred you, Josh. You really were Man of the Match!'

'It was teamwork,' muttered poor Josh.

Nobody doubted Josh had scored all three goals. Nobody had seen anyone else near the ball each time it found its mark. Everyone was ecstatic and Josh was their hero. He got changed in bewilderment. His team had won. He was a hero. But all he could feel was disappointment and confusion.

As they shared biscuits and hot chocolate with the St Luke's players, Josh looked around. None of their team seemed anything but resigned to their defeat. None of them looked as if they had been playing any crafty games – only straight soccer. Josh had watched everyone's feet as they walked into the building at the close of the match. Nobody's boot lace was untied apart from his own. Whoever had kicked the ball must have found time to retie their lace.

'Here's our star striker,' Mr Briggs told Josh's mother when she arrived later.

He patted Josh's back as the boy climbed into his mother's car. It was dark now and the thick fog swirled in the glow of the car's headlights.

'And his sister's going to star in the panto,' Josh's mother beamed. 'I'm proud of the pair of them.'

Josh let Mr Briggs close the car door and they set off home. Josh felt his mother's sideways glances as she drove. He guessed he did not look like a hero. Most likely he looked as sad and lost as he felt.

'Tired?'

Josh nodded. He felt no pride in the victory that had been attributed to him. Why had nobody else seen the phantom scorer? Why did they all think it was him? He felt glad his mother and sister hadn't been there. They would have seen it wasn't him who had scored. Then Josh remembered the photographer.

'Mum, will you make sure you get the *Echo* tomorrow?'

'It's delivered, silly,' said his mother.

'Well, please don't chuck it out till I've looked at the sports page,' said Josh.

*

Thankfully the next day was Saturday. Josh did not have to go to school and face his friends' misplaced praise. When the paper came, he turned straight to the sports page. There was the photograph, under the caption, 'HAT-TRICK HERO!' Josh stared in disbelief. There was a picture of him, kicking the ball. Hazy in the background the goalposts were just visible, framing the shadowy figure of the startled St Luke's goalie as he dived in the wrong direction. Underneath was a description of the action, praising both teams for their tenacity and courage in difficult conditions.

'I thought this was a football match, not a war!' Josh's mother commented, as she looked over her son's shoulder.

Josh looked hard at the action photograph. It was him all right. There was his boot in the air, with its dangling lace. And there was the ball curving away to land smack between the goalposts.

He was still staring at the page when the doorbell rang. It was Mr Williamson, an elderly man who lived a few doors away. He had lived there for years and was a good friend of Josh's family. He was waving a copy of the *Echo*.

'Your son's a chip off the old block, isn't he?' the old man chuckled. 'Congratulations, Josh,' he added, seeing Josh appear behind his mother.

'Come in,' she said. 'I'm glad someone else is as excited as I am. Josh seems to be taking it all in his stride.'

'What's a "chip off the old block"?' Josh asked.

The old man laughed. 'You're like your grandad Jim,' he explained. 'I was at school with him, you know. We were best mates and forever kicking a ball around. We played in the streets then, when there

10

weren't so many cars about. I reckon you take after him, lad.'

'I never knew him,' said Josh.

'You look just like him at the same age. Funny thing is,' he went on, 'I remember playing in a game just like this one. It's almost like history repeating itself. It was Jim's first inter-school match – and down came the fog. November it was, too. We won the game, two–nil, and your grandad scored both goals. But old Jim, he never forgot that match. You want to know why?' Josh nodded. His eyes were fixed on his neighbour's face. 'Well, when Jim's second goal put us in the lead, the ref blew his whistle on us. Stopped the match there and then. We'd won, but Jim never felt satisfied. He always said the blooming fog stopped him getting his hat-trick.' The old man laughed. 'Seems you've done it for him.'

For a minute Josh didn't speak. He had forgotten that his grandad's name was Jim. That was what Mr Henry had called Josh by mistake yesterday. Then he remembered the football rolling across the carpet to his side in the night.

Josh's mother was looking at him.

'You're right,' she said. 'He does look a lot like his grandad at that age. Hang on a minute, I've got a photo somewhere.'

She pulled an old shoebox from the cupboard and began to rummage through its contents. It was full of old envelopes and postcards with old-fashioned postage stamps. Black and white photographs were scattered amongst them. At last she pulled out a rather dog-eared print.

'Here we are,' she said, showing the old man. 'He's even in his school football strip.'

'Eh, up – that makes me feel old,' he said. 'There's Jim. How old? Eleven, maybe? And look – his boot lace is undone as usual. Just like yours, Josh!'

He handed Josh the photo. Josh had only seen pictures of his grandad as an adult. In this picture there was a boy looking up at him. The photograph was black and white, just like his own picture in today's paper and, for a second, Josh felt as if he was looking at a picture of himself. Jim had the same slim build as Josh; the same straight blond hair and the same eyes, that smiled up at him. Josh smiled back.

'Hat-trick hero,' he said.

Fixer

Anthony Masters

Jack rolled over on the muddy ground in the goal mouth, hugging the ball tight as Clapham United's fans roared their applause.

'Brilliant save!' yelled Rob as Jack struggled to his feet. He'd done it again. How long was his luck going to last?

But surely it wasn't luck, was it? It was skill. Ted Gill, United's coach, had told him that over and over again.

'Remember you've got talent. Luck isn't in it.' Ted had been almost impatient, for Jack never thought much of himself. Now Ted was cheering hard.

But Jack's elation died away as Barney Dexter's big, confident smile swam into his mind. 'You'll fix next Saturday's final, Jack. You'll let Albion in.'

Today was a friendly. It didn't matter to Barney. But next week did. If Jack couldn't fix the match against Wimbledon Albion, Barney would fix *him*. And then what would Mum think when she found out he'd been shoplifting?

'What's the matter?' asked Rob as they ran to the changing rooms after the match. 'You look like you've let 'em all in, not kept 'em all out.'

'I'm knackered,' was all Jack could say, and Rob

stared after him in surprise as he grabbed his bike and began the long ride home.

Jack didn't want to hurt his mother. She had been hurt already – hurt so badly by the drunken driver that she had been in a wheelchair ever since. The man had driven off, leaving her unconscious, but the police had eventually tracked him down. He had got off with a heavy fine and two years' ban. That wasn't enough for Jack. He would like to have killed him.

So much had gone wrong for his mother. Dad had walked out long ago, and had never contacted either of them again. Then there had been the accident that had left her paralysed.

Now Jack was going to give her a final blow.

As he cycled down the hill he remembered the amazing news that Ted Gill had given him a few weeks ago.

'You're going to be picked for the training scheme. I reckon you should be proud of yourself, Jack. Of course there's the coaching fees and the travel expenses . . .' Ted had looked at him anxiously. 'What with your mum and all . . .' He had paused, wondering how to go on. 'Will you have any problem about the money?'

You bet I will, Jack had thought. Even with all Mum's allowances we're always flat broke. But aloud he'd said, 'I'll manage.'

Jack knew that Mum wouldn't be able to afford the fees. He already had an early morning paper round and had tried to get the evening one, but had lost out to Tim Hawkins. So Jack had decided to start shoplifting, reckoning that if he managed to steal food, Mum would have enough money left to pay for his football training.

Jack wasn't dishonest by nature. In fact, he had never even contemplated doing such a terrible thing in his life. But there seemed no alternative.

'I've got the evening newspaper round,' he had lied to his mother when he got home. 'I can get some of the shopping with that if you can afford to pay my coaching fees out of your allowance.'

His mother, delighted and proud, had only one worry. 'You'll be exhausted. Two newspaper rounds – and then all that shopping.'

But Jack had told her the cycling would keep him fit, and eventually she had been satisfied.

He had hated lying to her and he had hated shop-lifting. But once Jack had stolen a pot of jam and a couple of tins of baked beans, the conscience that usually gave him a hard time seemed to get buried deep inside.

Jack took a shoulder bag to the supermarket, putting a few stolen items inside whilst the rest that he was actually going to pay for went straight into the trolley. It was too easy. What's more, he was well-known at the supermarket. After all, he'd been shopping here for the last two years and most of the checkout staff knew about his mother's accident. No one suspected him. Everyone thought he was a hero.

Jack had even begun to salve his conscience by convincing himself that he had every right to steal. The supermarket was a huge chain. They would never miss a few stolen goods. Mum was paralysed. They had no money. It was all he could do. There was no alternative.

'I can afford your training money,' Mum had reassured Jack as they had their tea. 'So when do you start?'

'After the final. The final we're going to win. We'll take Albion. No bother.'

Later, he had helped her out of her wheelchair and into bed as he did every night. Mum had got so thin that she was very easy to lift. He'd do the same in the morning. It always terrified him.

'Got you!' Barney Dexter had been holding a small camera.

Jack had gazed at him in horror. He'd forgotten that Barney was a shelf-filler in the evenings. A year older than Jack, he was one of the school's worst bullies.

'What are you talking about?'

'I saw you putting stuff in that bag last night so I decided to bring in the camera my granny gave me for Christmas.' His grin had widened. 'It's a Polaroid. Look at you then.'

He had held up the print, which showed Jack furtively snatching a tin of grapefruit segments from the shelf.

'So what?' Desperately he had tried to brazen it out.

'Where is it then? I don't see the tin in your trolley.'

'I must have made a mistake,' Jack had spluttered, his face reddening, the sweat standing out on his forehead, his heart hammering so much that it hurt.

'It's in your bag.'

'Keep your voice down.'

'Only if you show me.'

Jack had paused, panic blinding him, not knowing what to do.

Of course the tin was in his shoulder bag and so were several others, as well as half a pound of sausages.

'All right,' he had muttered, fighting back the

desperate tears, trying to keep control. 'What are you going to do?'

'It's more like what *you're* going to do, Jack.'

Barney had begun to replenish the stocks of canned fruit while Jack stood miserably beside him.

'You know my brother Warren?'

Jack had nodded. Warren was in his year. He was also the star striker for Wimbledon Albion, the team Clapham needed to beat at the final on Saturday. A dreadful flicker of understanding had raced across Jack's mind.

Barney had looked up, his grin malicious. 'I can see you're beginning to get the message.'

Jack had been determined he wasn't. 'I don't get you.'

'Try harder. You're going to let Warren in, aren't you?'

'He won't get near me.'

'Yes, he will. And you're going to let him in. Albion are going to win!'

'They're not!'

'Because you're going to fix the match. And if you don't, I'll take these prints to the manager here.'

'That doesn't prove a thing.'

'Didn't you hear what I said, thicko? I said – prints. In the plural, right?' Barney had reached into the pocket of his overall and held the second instant photograph close to Jack's eyes. This one all too clearly showed him putting a can of beans into his black shoulder bag.

'Get me?'

'Got you,' Jack had said, feeling sick.

'Of course, if you let Warren in I won't show them to anyone.'

Jack had tried to make a grab for the print, but Barney had been too quick for him, shoving it back into his pocket.

Without thinking of the consequences Jack had bunched his fists.

'Don't start anything,' Barney had said quietly. 'If you do, you'll give yourself away.'

Jack had walked home, his bag of stolen goods over his shoulder and the ones he hadn't stolen in two large plastic bags. What was he going to do, he had wondered. Barney Dexter had him completely in his power. If he was nicked for shoplifting what would Mum say? What would it do to her?

'Everything comes in threes,' she had once said bitterly. Jack had reminded her that it hadn't.

'Not yet,' she had replied gloomily.

Dad walking out. The drunk driver. And now her only son on a shoplifting charge. Who said everything didn't come in threes?

With two days to go to the match, Jack found that he couldn't sleep and was becoming increasingly irritable. He even took it out on Mum.

'It's the big one on Saturday,' she said enthusiastically over breakfast. 'Aren't you nervous?'

'Not really.' Jack's voice was flat as he pushed his cornflakes round his plate.

'You seem to have lost your appetite.'

No wonder, he thought. He was eating cornflakes from one of the miniature packets he'd nicked. He could hardly get them down without choking.

'I may be able to get to watch the match for once. Mrs Jennings said she'd bring me down.'

'I wouldn't bother.'

'Don't you want me there?' She was instantly hurt.

Jack stood up, knowing how badly he was upsetting her, yet knowing how much more deeply upset she would be if he was found out. He'd *have* to let the shots in. He'd *have* to fix the match. He didn't have any choice.

But suppose Barney Dexter didn't destroy those prints? Suppose he went on blackmailing him for ever?

'I've got to get to school.'

'But you're early.'

'Bye, Mum.' He gave her a peck on the cheek and was gone.

Looking back, Jack saw his mother gazing after him like a wounded animal.

Barney was waiting for him by the lockers.

'You're going to fix the match, aren't you?'

A dark red mist seemed to have drifted into Jack's eyes, and inside he felt tight as a drum – as if he could hardly breathe. 'Please,' he whispered. 'I *can't.*'

'Your mum's not going to like you being done for shoplifting, is she?' Barney grinned. 'Not after all she's been through.'

The red mist darkened until it was so dense that Jack could hardly see. 'You leave her out of it.'

'The police won't.'

Barney was taller than Jack and much stronger. Nevertheless, Jack threw himself at him, punching and kicking, yelling abuse.

As the blows connected, Barney was forced back against the lockers, head down, protecting his face with his hands, too afraid to fight back, as an interested crowd began to collect.

Then Rob arrived, broke through the spectators and grabbed Jack round the waist, pulling him away from

Barney, trying to defuse the violence. Jack struggled in his grasp.

Then the bell went and the crowd immediately dispersed.

'I'll get you for that,' Barney muttered as he limped away. 'You see if I don't.'

But Jack knew he already had.

'What on earth was that all about?' Rob asked.

'He said something about my mum.'

'What?'

'It doesn't matter.'

'You know what he's like.'

'You bet I do.'

'You don't want to start getting into fights. Not with the match a couple of days away.'

'Get off my back!' yelled Jack, all his frustrated rage and anxiety returning.

'I'm only trying to help.' Rob looked like Mum. Hurt and bewildered.

'Don't bother.' Jack ran off in the direction of his tutor group.

Jack stood in the goal mouth, poised and ready. The last couple of nights had been really bad and he had hardly slept at all for worrying about what he was going to have to do. He hadn't been near the supermarket, getting what they needed from the more expensive corner shop, and Mum had been surprised at how quickly her allowance had been used up again.

'I thought things would be easier with that extra money from your evening news round, but it doesn't seem to be making as much difference as I thought,' she had said last night, totting up her petty cash book.

Immediately Jack's lies had got more complicated. 'I've lost the round, Mum. I couldn't face telling you.'

'But how?' She had been bewildered again. 'Mr Dawson's always thought so highly of you.'

'I was a bit late the other night and he was in a bad mood. So he took the round off me and gave it to Will Rogers.'

'That's not fair.'

'It doesn't matter.'

'Anyway,' she had said. 'I'm glad.'

'Glad?' Now it had been Jack's turn to be bewildered.

'It was too much for you. Draining all your energy. It could even have wrecked the match.'

The match was wrecked already, thought Jack as Warren Dexter came pounding towards him.

'What's the matter, Jack?' Ted Gill was furious with him at half-time. So were the rest of the team as they gathered together for a briefing. But the briefing was more like an inquest.

Only Rob looked concerned. Everybody else was out for his blood.

'You've got to wake up!' snapped Ted Gill. 'You let two easy ones through. Why?'

'I don't know.'

'You looked like a performing seal,' commented Dean Harrison.

'More like a ballet dancer,' added Jake Thompson nastily.

'Who asked for *your* views?' Ted Gill turned on them angrily. 'We all have our off days. Jack's having one of his. But we're going to save the match, lads, and I'll tell you how.'

As Ted Gill talked tactics, Jack felt relieved that his mother hadn't turned up to watch him blow the game away. Not so far, anyway.

Ted had been right. The shots had been too easy to let through. Far too easy. What was he going to do? Everyone would soon realize he was fixing the match. If anyone was having an off day, it had to be Warren Dexter.

'Your mum's here,' said Rob as they walked back to the pitch.

Sure enough, she was on the sideline in her wheelchair, barely able to stop giving Jack a wave. Her appearance was the final blow.

Mrs Jennings was hovering behind his mother. Maybe she'd been late or her car had packed up.

'Show your mum what you can do,' said Rob. 'Don't let her down.'

Something clicked in Jack's mind. Of course he couldn't let Mum down. Not now. Not on the field. She was going to be properly let down later, he told himself. Even if he let the shots through he'd never get Barney off his back. He knew that now. How was she going to like having a thief for a son?

He glanced towards the sideline. Barney Dexter had been standing there all the way through the first half, a smile fixed on his big meaty face.

Now Jack was going to blow that stupid grin away.

Warren Dexter was on him again, running towards the goal mouth, manoeuvring the muddy ball with rather more skill while the Albion supporters went mad, cheering and shouting, chanting his name.

Jack gazed at him intently, trying to read his mind, watching his feet. Where was he going to put the ball?

Had his coach given him a talking-to? He seemed much more on form. For a moment Jack thought he knew what Warren's tactics were going to be. Then, just in time, he realized he was trying to fool him.

Jack dived as the ball shot towards the net.

Now it was the turn of the Clapham United supporters to go wild as Jack made his save, scrambled to his feet and kicked the ball out of the penalty area.

'Well saved, Jack!' shouted Ted Gill. He was standing next to Barney Dexter, whose grin was still firmly in place.

Jack knew that Barney thought the save was just part of his fixing strategy. Let in two, keep one out, let in the others, so they would look like mistakes. But now Barney had another think coming.

Jack turned to glance at his mother, who was clapping delightedly and shouting his name.

His love for her welled up inside him with such intensity that he could feel tears pricking at the backs of his eyes.

What was the best of the two options? Let her see him fail as United's goalie? Or see him branded as a thief?

Jack saved two more shots in spectacular style. His sudden return to form made Clapham United attack much more aggressively and soon there were two balls in Albion's net and it looked as if the game might end in a draw.

Then, just before the referee blew the whistle for full-time, Rob scored.

As the Clapham supporters cheered for all they were worth, Jack turned to face Barney Dexter. He was in exactly the same position on the sideline, the grin still on his face. But he was holding up a couple of prints and Jack knew exactly what they were, and what he was going to do with them.

Then he had a sudden and very risky idea.

'You did well, Jack. You really did well.' His mother looked younger, full of life – exhausted but also enormously excited. He had not seen her this way for a long, long time.

Her praise was worth more than Ted Gill's, more than his team-mates', more than Rob's.

But Jack realized that if his plan didn't work out – and it was a long shot – then his mother might be badly hurt once too often.

'I'll be home soon, Mum. I'm just going to . . .' he hesitated, 'cycle back with Rob. We want to talk over the game.'

'I bet you do, love,' she said. 'But don't be too self-critical. You were wonderful.'

Wonderful? he thought. I'm not wonderful. I'm a thief.

Jack found Rob in the changing room.

'I want to talk to you.'

'What about?' Rob looked at Jack curiously.

'My sudden return to form.'

'Warren seemed to have the same problem in the first half. But what went wrong with you?'

Slowly, hesitantly, Jack began to tell him.

When he had finished, there was a long silence.

'Come on then,' said Jack. 'Say you despise me.'

'I don't.'

'You should.'

'You were set up and you fought back. Now you've got me to help you.'

'We want to see the manager.' Rob was insistent.

'What about?' The supervisor looked put out.

'It's important.'

'Can't I help?'

'Not really.' Jack was trembling.

'Very well. Step this way – but I hope you're not going to waste Mr Johnson's time.'

'No,' said Rob. 'We're not going to waste a second of it.'

The office was small and functional with a few chairs, a couple of filing cabinets, a telephone and a nameplate on the desk: *Graham Johnson.*

The manager was young and friendly, unlike the supervisor, who snapped the door shut disapprovingly.

'Do sit down,' he told the boys.

They did as he said. A long silence developed. Jack's mouth was so dry that he could hardly bring the words out. Then he forced himself.

'I – I took some stuff,' he stuttered. 'Because my mum's ill. We don't have enough money. I've been picked for the football training scheme. I can't afford the fees. She's in a wheelchair. Mum can't afford the fees either. I told her I had a round. A newspaper round. But I didn't. I never had one – at least, I did in the mornings, but not in the evenings.' Jack came to a shuddering halt, knowing that he wasn't making any sense.

He glanced at Rob but he was looking away, red in the face with embarrassment.

Jack plunged on.

'Barney Dexter – he took these photographs. Like of me nicking stuff. He said if I didn't fix the match, he'd take them to you.'

As if on cue, there was a knock at the door and the supervisor reappeared, looking even more irritated.

25

'Yes. What is it now?' asked Graham Johnson briskly.

'There's someone else to see you.'

'Who is it?'

'Guy called Dexter. Works for us part time as a shelf-filler. Says he's got something you should see.'

'Tell him I'm busy right now.' The supervisor closed the door reluctantly.

'Now look,' said Graham Johnson. 'Why don't we begin all over again? I didn't really understand what you were on about.'

This time Jack spoke more slowly and clearly. But as he told his story, he could already imagine telling it again to a policeman.

When he had finished, all Graham Johnson could say was, 'I see.' The silence filled the room like cold lead. Then he spoke again. 'I think you've been punished enough, don't you?'

Jack gazed at him, unable to believe his ears.

'Our usual policy is to prosecute shoplifters, but I'm not going to this time. In fact, I'm going to ask you if you'd like a job. There's a vacancy going.'

'Is there?' Waves of shock filled him, and Jack could hardly grasp what was being said. Rob was looking incredulous.

'It's just come up. A shelf-filler.'

'But I'd be working with—'

'Dexter's leaving.'

'Is he?'

Graham Johnson got to his feet. 'So how did the match go then?' he asked.

As Rob and Jack left the manager's office, feeling not only bewildered but amazingly relieved, they saw

Barney Dexter standing outside, the prints clasped in his hand, his grin unusually strained.

'Mr Dexter?' Graham Johnson's voice was cold. 'Would you like to come in?'

'Thanks for coming with me, Rob,' said Jack as they walked over to their bikes.

'That's all right.'

'I can hardly believe what's happened.'

'Neither can I. But what are you going to tell your mum?'

'The truth.'

'Is that a good idea?'

'If I don't, Barney might get to her first. If I can tell you and the manager, I can tell Mum.'

'Want me to come?'

'Not this time.'

Rob nodded, and Jack knew that he understood.

When Jack got back home, Mum was in the kitchen, doing all she could to make tea on her own. She was still full of excitement.

'You were great, Jack,' she said.

'I wasn't till you turned up.'

'I'm sorry. Mrs Jennings' car broke down and—'

'You saved me. And then I stopped the shots. But I've got something to tell you – something I'm ashamed of.'

She looked up at him calmly. 'What is it, Jack?'

Slowly, and then more confidently, he began to tell his mother what had happened.

A Dog Called Lineker

Eric Johns

'We're going to have a knock-out competition,' Claire
announced.

'Which teams are playing?' Speed wanted to know.

'Mine and Russo's.'

'What d'you mean, *your* team?' Speed asked indignantly.

'It's my idea, so I'm the captain,' Claire told him.

'But you're the goalkeeper,' Speed objected. 'Goalies
can't be captain.'

'Peter Schmeichel is sometimes,' Claire said.

'We've never had a captain before,' Danny put in.
'We've all just *played*.'

'Well, this time we're playing Russo's mob, so we
need a captain and that's me. Does anyone not want
to play?'

The five players who suddenly found themselves in
Claire's team looked at her. She was short and broad
with bristling fair hair which was about one centimetre
long all over. She had scabby knees, torn shorts and
trainers with splits in them.

Dave, Nicky and Sam glanced at each other and
shrugged. They didn't really care who was captain or
whether there was one at all. Claire glared at Speed
and Danny.

'Even if we let you be captain,' Speed said, 'it won't

make any difference because you'll be too far away in goal to tell us what to do.'

'I'll be thinking up tactics so we win,' Claire said firmly.

It was the summer holidays. The weather was hot and Claire and her friends had nothing much to do. They met each morning on the recreation ground and messed about on the swings and other apparatus, or kicked a football about.

It was while the others were taking shots at her in goal, that Claire came up with the idea of a knock-out competition. What she wanted was something more exciting than just stopping endless shots she could see coming a mile off.

'So who's in this competition besides us and Russo?' Danny asked.

'That's all. There aren't any other teams round here.'

'You can't have a competition with only two teams,' Speed told her.

'Why not?'

'It's not a competition, just a game.'

'Well, it's the final,' Claire decided. 'The Summer Cup Final.'

Speed looked doubtful. 'You know what Russo's lot are like,' he told the others. 'If it looks like we might win, they'll start to cheat.'

'We'll just have to watch them all the time,' Claire said.

'Have you asked Russo whether he even wants to play?' Danny asked.

'Not yet. I was just going to ask him now.'

The six of them set off to see Russo's team. They played at the other end of the recreation ground – the end with the goalposts. No one knew why the recreation ground only had one set of goalposts, but everyone knew why Russo and his team had to have that end. They thought they were better than anyone else. Claire's team made do with bags or coats for goalposts.

As they approached Russo's team, Claire looked with envy at the kit they wore. All six of them were dressed in the latest strip for Manchester United. Not that she wanted that strip for herself. She supported Southampton (just to be different), but it would have been nice to have a proper strip. Her team looked like tramps.

'Look at them!' Speed snorted. 'As soon as they see us they start acting big.'

It was true. Mel, Russo's best striker, took a shot at goal, missed and threw up his arms in despair as if he'd been cheated out of the goal of the season by an unexpected earthquake.

'What d'you want?' Russo wanted to know, sounding as if he thought they'd come to steal his goalposts.

'We thought you might like a game,' Claire told him.

'Unless you don't want to risk getting your kit dirty,' Speed added, just to encourage them to accept the challenge.

'We might,' Russo said, and turned to his team. 'What d'you say? D'you fancy teaching them how to play?'

'All right by me,' Tone, their goalkeeper, said. 'So long as they agree to stop when it gets to twenty–nil. It'd get boring after that.'

'Yeah,' Mel put in. 'We'd better decide on the rules before we start, so they can't change them after.'

The teams spent some time sorting out the rules and

agreed to play the next morning. That would give them enough time to work out tactics.

'Right,' Claire said when they'd returned to their end of the recreation ground. 'Speed and Danny, you're strikers. Nicky and Sam, you'll mark Russo and Mel, and Dave, you'll be sweeper. OK?' she asked.

No one argued about the positions because those were the positions they always played in.

'We'll have a practice,' Claire said. 'Speed, you be Russo, and Danny be Mel.'

Speed and Danny took the ball up the field, then started passing to each other as they returned to attack. Speed ran easily round Nicky, and Danny avoided Sam without difficulty. That only left Dave. They switched the ball between them to get past him, and Danny shot. It was only a brilliant save by Claire that prevented a goal.

Claire could see that her team's defence was its weak point. Nicky and Sam were doing what she told them, but somehow it didn't look right. It wasn't the way they usually played. Perhaps, she thought, proper tactics, like marking, only worked with real teams where everyone was used to doing what they were supposed to. She sighed. 'All right. Forget about marking. Play the way you usually do,' she told her defence.

The three defenders smiled happily. Claire threw the ball to Dave to clear. Nicky and Sam closed in on him, and the three of them raced past Speed and Danny with the ball hidden somewhere in the middle of them. They kicked the ball away and ran back to take up defensive positions while Speed went to fetch it.

Speed and Danny attacked. Nicky deflected the ball, and the three defenders closed in on it. Claire frowned.

The three of them were like three different bits of one player instead of three different players. They always raced in the same direction like lemmings. That was what her defence reminded her of – lemmings.

'We'll call ourselves the Lemmings,' Claire shouted down the field.

'Why?' Danny asked.

'It just seems right.'

'I agree,' Speed said glumly.

Just then Claire heard her mum's voice echo across the recreation ground. 'Claire! Dinner.'

'Are we going to practise this afternoon?' Claire asked her team.

No one seemed very enthusiastic.

'All right. We'll meet tomorrow, half an hour before the game for a warm-up.'

She trotted off to her mum. Lineker, her black and white collie dog, was standing on his back legs straining against his lead as he tried to get to her. Her mum let him go and he charged at Claire. She dived sideways and grabbed the lead as it whipped past. She was pulled along until Lineker decided she was too heavy and came back to lick her instead.

'Look at the state of you,' Claire's mum said. That was what she usually said instead of hello.

Claire was a mess because she was a fearless goalie. She never hesitated to take the ball away from a striker. Even in summer, when the ground was as hard as the flapjacks they cooked at school, she still threw herself in the path of anyone who jinked past her defence.

After lunch, Claire practised goalkeeping. The garage wall was the goal and Lineker was striker. Claire threw the ball into the air and let Lineker hit it with his nose. He never missed, but Claire never knew which way the ball was going to go. Lineker definitely tried to punt it back to her. He understood the game all right, but accuracy wasn't his strong point. Claire didn't mind. It was good practice not knowing which angle the ball was going to come from.

'You must have a nose like an old boot,' Claire told Lineker, after twenty minutes. She always worried that he'd hurt his nose, but he never seemed to. 'I don't think the Lemmings have got much chance tomorrow,' she admitted to him. 'I wish you could play.'

Next morning, the Lemmings met as arranged. Speed and Danny did muscle-stretching exercises, Claire bounced up and down in the space between the two piles of jackets and bags, and Dave, Nicky and Sam ran round in circles like lemmings looking for a cliff to jump off.

At the other end of the pitch, Russo's team fired balls at Tone who was in goal. Claire looked at them enviously. They had four proper leather footballs to practise with, while all her team had was a plastic one which was starting to go down since Lineker had tried to bite it.

Claire sighed. The Lemmings' chances seemed to be about zero. Things weren't going to turn out anything like she'd imagined. There were no roaring crowds, no floodlights, no scouts from famous clubs who'd been tipped off about the unknown goalie everyone was talking about.

Russo jogged down the pitch. 'You ready, then?'

'Yeah. We're warmed up,' Claire said, trying to sound professional.

'We'll use one of our balls,' Russo decided, glancing away from Claire's ball as if it hurt his eyes.

The two teams spread out. The ground was far too big for teams of six players. If anyone got away with the ball he'd have so much space he'd never be caught. It would be striker against goalie.

'OK,' Russo said. 'You call.' He tossed a coin.

'Heads,' Claire said.

'It's tails,' Mel yelled.

'We kick off,' Russo decided.

Claire looked at his team. They all seemed bigger than her players.

Russo kicked the ball forward, and Mel ran deep into the Lemmings' half. He and Russo swung the ball from wing to wing, and Claire winced as Dave, Nicky and Sam charged from one side of the pitch to the other. She knew what was going to happen. Any second now, Russo or Mel was going to make a run at goal and her defence would be on the other side of the field.

It was Mel who did it. Claire came out of her goal to narrow the angle of his shot. Dave, Nicky and Sam came charging back but were far too late. She was lucky, though. Mel's shot was just to her left and at an easy height. Claire dived and pushed it wide.

Russo's team all yelled, 'Corner!'

Two of his defence came up to help the attack, and Speed dropped back. Mel took the kick. Claire had to admit that it was a good ball. It came over high and dropped in the centre of the goal mouth. Dave, Nicky and Sam closed round it so that Claire couldn't see where it was. They all lashed wildly at the ball and got in each other's way. Suddenly, the ball rocketed out of the scrimmage and shot towards Danny who

35

was standing near the halfway line. Claire yelled at him.

Danny pounced on the ball and sprinted away. It ran easily, always a pace in front of him. There was plenty of space. The over-confident Russo's team had left him unmarked. By the time the one defender still in their half had woken up to what was happening, Danny was too far ahead to catch. He ran right up to the goalie, dribbled past him and put the ball between the posts.

The Lemmings whooped in triumph. Dave, Nicky and Sam ran round in circles chanting, 'One–nil. One–nil!' Claire tried to look as though this was what she had planned. What she was really thinking was that they couldn't be that lucky again.

Russo didn't look pleased. 'What d'you think you're playing at?' he shouted at his defender.

'He was asleep,' Mel said scornfully.

As soon as they started again, Russo sprinted straight down the pitch. Mel lobbed a long ball to him. He held onto it until Dave, Nicky and Sam, in their usual tight group, were almost on top of him, then he ran round them contemptuously. Claire groaned to herself. Russo charged towards her. She ran forward, but knew that this time she would not be as lucky as before.

Russo checked his pace and swung his foot at the ball. It was going slightly quicker than he thought, and when he hit it he was at full stretch. The ball rose in the air and soared over Claire's head.

'Goal!' Mel roared.

'That wasn't a goal,' Claire objected. 'It was too high. It would have gone over the bar.'

'There isn't any bar,' Russo said calmly.

Speed came jogging back to support his captain. 'You've still got to keep the ball low enough so's it would go under the bar, if there was one.'

'You didn't say that when we agreed the rules,' Mel said.

'We didn't need to,' Claire objected. 'It's obvious.'

'Oh, yeah. It's obvious now we've scored a goal,' Russo said mockingly, 'but you should have thought of it before.'

'Either that's a goal or we don't play any more,' Mel told them.

'You can't change the rules after the game's started,' Russo added, smirking.

Russo's team jogged back to their positions.

'I told you they wouldn't play fair,' Speed said glumly.

From then on, Russo's team were all over the Lemmings. Claire made several heroic saves, but it was only going to be a matter of time before a ball came out of a goal area scrimmage and got past her.

It happened when, not for the first time, Dave, Nicky and Sam were between her and the ball. Mel came charging at the ball, obviously intending to blast it straight at the three defenders. Acting like true lemmings they fled out of the path of the shot, and the ball hurtled through the space they'd left and past Claire before she even saw it.

'That was typical Lemming defence,' Claire muttered as she jogged to fetch the ball which did not stop until it hit the wire fence at the edge of the recreation ground. 'As good as an own goal,' she added.

She felt fed up. This was not what she'd hoped for. She'd known her team were unlikely to win, but she'd hoped they would look a bit more like a proper team.

In the distance Russo's team were laughing and jumping on each other in triumph.

They kicked off again. Speed tapped the ball to Danny and he passed back to Dave who was supposed to pass forward again to whoever of them wasn't marked.

Claire stood in her goal and watched Speed and Danny run up the field on either wing. Two defenders ran out to mark them, while the third stayed in front of the penalty area. Russo and Mel ran towards her, ready to be fed a ball once the defence had stopped the attack. Claire nodded approvingly. Russo's team looked as though they knew what football was all about, even though they did cheat.

She waited for Dave to pass to Speed or Danny. He didn't. Instead, the three Lemming defenders closed round the ball and headed down the centre of the field towards the defender on the edge of the penalty area. Even at that distance Claire could see the puzzled expression on his face. Standing in goal with no defence, she knew how he felt. Her team's tactics made her feel like switching to tiddly-winks.

Dave, Nicky and Sam looked like three lemmings who had suddenly spotted the edge of a cliff and did not intend to stop until they'd thrown themselves over it. They swerved round the defender, who seemed unable to decide which of them had the ball or which way it was going to go. The goalkeeper seemed just as puzzled. The ball bounced around between the three Lemmings like a ball stuck between three posts in a pinball machine.

The goalkeeper threw himself in their path, but the three of them curved round him as if each of them knew exactly which way the other two were going to go.

Somehow, the three of them dribbled the ball over the goal line.

'Goal!' the Lemmings screamed. Claire, Speed and Danny rushed to congratulate the three defenders. They leapt up and down in the centre of the pitch.

'Two–all! Two–all!' they chanted.

'Come on!' Russo shouted. 'Let's get on with the game.'

'Or you'll be penalized for time-wasting,' Mel added.

Claire jogged back to her goal mouth. Her team might not look much like real footballers but they were holding their own against a team with proper kit and four leather footballs between them.

When Russo's team kicked off, Mel made a bad pass and Danny won the ball. He ran round a defender and crossed to Speed.

'Pass back. Quick!' Claire shouted. Then she saw a movement by the gate to the recreation ground. It was her mum with Lineker on his lead.

'Oh, no,' she moaned. 'Don't call me to go in. Not now we've got a chance to score.'

They'd agreed at the start that if either captain had to go home, that would be the final whistle.

It would be just her luck to be called now.

Speed and Danny were in front of the goal. There was only one defender and the goalkeeper. Danny struck the ball. It was a beautiful shot, heading towards the top corner of the goal. The keeper ran off his line and jumped. He just got a fist to the ball. It was a brilliant save. Claire wished she'd made it.

The ball arced up high and dropped towards the

edge of the penalty area. At that moment Claire glimpsed a black shape streaking across the pitch.

'Lineker!' she exclaimed.

The dog was going so fast that his lead was flying straight out behind him. He hit the ball with his leather-hard nose. It was the finest shot of his career.

The ball cannoned into the bottom corner of the goal.

'Goal!' Dave, Nicky and Sam yelled, laughing. They were joking, but suddenly an idea came to Claire – an idea that would teach Russo to play fair.

'Goal!' she shouted. 'Goal! We're leading three–two!'

'Don't be stupid,' Russo said crossly. 'Dogs can't score goals.'

'Why not?' Claire demanded.

'It's against the rules.'

'You didn't say that when we agreed them,' Claire argued.

'Everyone *knows* dogs can't score,' Mel objected.

'Well, you should have said so before,' Speed told him. 'You can't change the rules after the game's started.'

'We'll abandon the game if you're going to be stupid,' Mel threatened.

'What's the matter?' Danny wanted to know. 'You scared you won't score another?'

'Right, let's show them,' Russo cried. 'You can have that goal and we'll still beat you.'

Just then a voice from the edge of the recreation ground called out, 'Coo-eee! Russell!'

Russo seemed to shrink.

Both teams turned to see where the voice had come from. Standing by the fence was a tall lady in a big, purple sunhat, a tight, green shirt, pink shorts and silver shoes with stiletto heels. She was waving at Russo.

'Russell, darling,' she called. 'It's time for lunch and your vitamin pills.'

'We'll finish this game another time,' Russo grunted, his ears turning as red as his shirt.

'If you go,' Claire said, 'the game ends – and we've won. That's what we agreed.'

Russo tried to shrug to show he didn't care, but his shoulders drooped defeatedly.

The Lemmings sportingly clapped the losing team off the pitch. They heard Russo say to the woman, 'I *told* you never to come up here!'

'D'you think that's his mum?' Speed asked, giggling.

'Poor old Russo,' Danny said. 'I've never felt sorry for him before.'

Claire ran over to her mum to tell her the result.

'I'm sorry about letting Lineker go,' her mum said apologetically. 'When he saw the ball he jerked the lead right out of my hand.'

'That's OK,' Claire said laughing. 'He was definitely Dog of the Match!'

Jessica's Brother

Gus Grenfell

'Keep your eye on the ball!' How many times had people yelled that at him? Well, they wouldn't need to this time.

The midfielder's hurried clearance was still high in the air, and Owen Foley fixed all his concentration on it. It was going to overshoot him so he backpedalled quickly, positioning himself for the header. He rose as the ball fell. His timing was perfect.

Crunch! The charge from the left caught him in mid-air. The opposing striker didn't look big enough to have such an impact on Owen, but he was knocked sideways like a skittle. He turned as he fell and landed front first, knocking the wind from his lungs. The striker gathered the ball, sidestepped the keeper and calmly side-footed into an empty net.

Owen lay there for a moment, then slowly hauled his lanky frame upright. He scraped the mud off his arms and pushed his sandy fair hair out of his eyes.

'Are you blind, Owen? Didn't you see him coming?' Chris, the goalkeeper, hands on hips, was staring at him angrily under the bill of his green baseball cap.

Owen said nothing. How could you keep your eye on the ball *and* on your opponent at the same time? He dragged himself dispiritedly to the edge of the D for the restart.

The whistle went a minute later, before Owen had really got his breath back. He turned and headed for the changing rooms, disappointed with the way he had performed. He had tried to play a sensible game, not be drawn out of position, but he seemed to have been stuck in the same spot most of the game.

He hadn't missed all his headers, and he'd made a few decent tackles, but he hadn't been very adventurous. He had tried to be solid and dependable in central defence, but he was afraid he'd ended up being dull.

Chris ran up and clapped him on the shoulder, his usual grin back in place, his baseball cap under one arm. Owen grinned back and punched his arm. No hard feelings; they were mates. After all, this was the pre-season trials, not a cup final.

It was all right for Chris, he had been a regular in the Under-12 team and there was no one to touch him, so his place in the Under-13s was assured. Owen had been convinced he was going to make it this time. Until now. The grin went. He felt like crying with frustration. It would be 'We'll let you know', and then the phone call saying, 'Sorry, I'm afraid we haven't got a place for you in the squad at present.' Again. Just like the other times.

There were other games still underway on nearby pitches. Some involved boys younger than him, some older, and, to judge from the shrill cries coming from a pitch over to the right, the girls – about to get their own team for the first time – were going through their paces.

Owen could see a familiar red head bobbing up in the middle of a bunch of players. Jessica, his sister, had insisted that if he could have a trial, so could she,

44

and Mum had taken her part, of course. So Dad had driven them all down. Embarrassing or what!

When he was changed, Owen walked over to the car park. Dad was in the car alone.

'Where's Mum?' he asked, sliding into the back seat.

'Still waiting for Jessica, I expect. How did you get on?'

'Not very well. I don't think I'll get in.' Owen couldn't trust himself to say anything else. He could feel his throat tightening.

'Never mind. I expect you did your best. We can't all be footballers.'

That was Dad all over. He was so easy going. He never seemed to get upset. Owen sometimes wished his father would shout at him, say what did he mean by not getting in the team, and if that was his best then it wasn't good enough. Then Owen could let go and shout back and get it all out of his system. Instead he had to bottle it all up and pretend it didn't matter.

Owen had read halfway through his copy of *Shoot* before Mum and Jessica appeared. Jessica was jumping up and down, and they were both grinning like Cheshire cats. A terrible thought occurred to him. Surely she couldn't have; he'd never considered it remotely possible. But a cold certainty was forming in the pit of his stomach. He didn't need to hear Jessica's jubilant announcement as they came within shouting distance.

'I'm in the squad, I'm in the squad!'

She rushed to the car, wrenched open the door, bounced onto the seat and flung her arms round him. 'Owen, I'm going to play for the Under-11s! They said I was ever so good, didn't they, Mum? They said I've got good ball skills and a solid left-foot shot, didn't they?'

Mum was pink-cheeked and breathless, almost as though she'd been playing herself. She was talking to Dad.

'Sorry we were so long,' she said. 'I've been talking to the manager and the other mums. Isn't it exciting? They want her to go for training twice a week. I said we could manage it.'

She paused and turned to the back seat.

'What do you think, Owen?'

Owen was busy trying to fight Jessica off.

'I'm sorry, I ought to have asked how you . . .'

The thundercloud on his face must have made it obvious.

'Oh, Owen, I'm so sorry, really I am.' She put her hand through the gap between the front seats and rested it on his knee. He tried to squirm away, but there was nowhere to go.

'Well, at least,' she said, 'you'll be able to be happy for Jessica.'

Happy for Jessica? That was the last thing he felt. At this moment he wished a great hole would open in the upholstery and swallow him.

School. Monday morning. At least it was a relief to be out of the house, away from all the excitement and Jessica-centred conversation.

What kind of boots should she have? 'Knee-length patent leather with high heels,' he'd said. Frowns all round. Not funny.

How would she look in the new yellow strip with red shorts? 'Blood and pus,' he'd said, deliberately jolting the table as Jessica had a spoonful of cornflakes almost in her mouth.

And a mouth guard. She'd need a mouth guard. 'A mouth guard?' He was scornful. 'Nobody suggested I should have a mouth guard. I suppose it doesn't matter if I get my teeth knocked right down my throat.'

Oh, and they were having a competition to find a name for the team. 'Barbies!' he'd said, leaving the room and slamming the door.

It was morning break, and Chris was coming towards him, holding a slightly out-of-shape football with most of its surface scuffed off, and gaps where the stitching had gone, like gaping underwear.

'Fancy a kick-around?' he said.

'Why not?' They ran out into the yard, gathering others as they went.

The yard at the front of the school had once been tennis courts and was surrounded at the back and sides by high, chain-link fencing. The wall of the school itself formed the other side.

Owen found himself attacking the school end, the goal between a drainpipe and a litter bin. Good. In his present mood he could just fancy belting the ball against a wall, and not having to bother about the finer points of the game.

Chris threw the ball in the air and there was a rush as it came to land, mainly from the few year seven boys who were allowed to play and were keen to impress. They'd only been at the school a week.

Owen stood back as the melee sorted itself out and the ball trickled loose. He hacked it towards the wall where Pete, the largest and laziest of his team-mates, was lounging. Pete didn't even need to lever himself off the wall or take his hands out of his pockets. He simply stuck out a leg and guided the ball into the goal area.

'One–nil!' Owen shouted. 'I bet we get twenty before the bell goes.'

'Bet you don't,' said Chris, kicking the ball from his hands. Nobody intercepted it. The chain link rattled and bulged.

'One–all!' It wasn't a game for midfielders.

Owen set off with the ball at his feet, taking advantage of the lack of touchlines, and did a mazy run round two other games going on in different parts of the yard, pursued by a gaggle of year sevens.

'Show-off!' Chris shouted.

Owen paused, taking stock, seeing if there was anyone to pass to. One of the year sevens nipped in front of him and took the ball off his toe. The cheek of it! Everybody laughed, which didn't improve Owen's mood at all. He ran after the kid, grabbed his arm and pulled him back.

'Hey, foul, ref!' the boy called.

Owen ignored him. That was another advantage of school yard soccer; no officials.

'Are you Jessica Foley's brother?' said the cheeky little year seven kid. 'My dad says she's the best lass he's ever seen play.'

Owen was seething. He eyed up the ball, bobbling unevenly on the pitted asphalt, and whacked it. The ball hit the bin with a clang and knocked it over, scattering crisp packets and coke cans in the goal mouth. The ball rebounded, still in play.

'Leave it!' Owen shouted, determined to quieten the laughter, and charged forward. He let fly with an uncontrolled swing. His foot went under the ball and sent it ballooning over the heads of his mates. And right through the library window.

It wasn't Owen's day.

And it got worse. Owen had a letter from the Deputy Head to hand over when he got home, which included a bill for the broken window. He'd thought of chucking it on the way back, except that the Deputy Head said he would ring to make sure it arrived and 'talk about the issue'. The ball had been confiscated as well, and they were banned from playing football in the yard. And he was on lunchtime litter duty for the rest of the week.

Dad was on the phone when he opened the door, talking in that smarmy voice he used for people like deputy heads. Yes, of course. He would take it out of Owen's pocket money. Yes, boys did need to learn how to act responsibly around the school. Traitor. Why didn't he tell the Deputy Head to stuff it and pay for the window himself? Some boys had dads like that.

Owen walked into the sitting room and wished he hadn't. Mum and Jessica were all in a tizz about football practice; they had to go in ten minutes. He slammed out and went upstairs to his room. He would get something to eat while they were out, then stay in his room all evening. Even if it did mean watching Monday evening football on the miserable little black and white telly they let him have.

He hadn't bargained on the invasion later. They came rushing upstairs and burst into his room as soon as they got back, ignoring the *Area 51 – Keep Out* sign he had on the door; ignoring the fact that he was watching the match.

Jessica was full of herself.

'I'm in the team!' she said, bouncing around as if she were on a pogo stick. 'I'm going to play for the Beacons.'

'The *what*?' Owen asked.

'The Beacons. Beamsley Beacons. That's our name. Yellow shirts, see? And there used to be a beacon on top of the hill outside the town. It sounds right. Don't you think it's good?'

'No, it's rubbish,' he said, scowling.

'Well, everybody else likes it. We're going to play Stanbury Sparx on Saturday. They've just formed as well. I can't wait.'

Dad was standing in the doorway now. 'What position do you play?' he asked.

'Oh, everywhere!' she replied, whirling round with her arms stretched out. 'I just watch what's going on and run to the best place.'

And after ten minutes you fall flat on your back, exhausted, Owen thought. Somehow he didn't think his sister was ready for total football. He moved his head to the left to see round her to the television, but she moved and blocked the screen again. He moved his head back.

'And I scored lots of goals in the game at the end, didn't I, Mum?' she said. 'How many was it?'

Mum laughed. 'I can't remember. Seven or eight?'

'The last one was the best. I ran all the way down the pitch.'

The increased tempo and pitch of the commentator's voice told Owen he had missed a goal.

'Do you mind?' he said, jumping up off the bed and pushing Jessica aside. 'I'm trying to watch the match.' He swore as he was just too late to catch the action replay.

There was a tense silence.

'Well! Sorry, I'm sure,' Mum said. 'We thought you'd be interested, that's all.'

'Well I'm not. OK?'

They withdrew, deflated.

He knew he hadn't heard the last of it. Mum would come up and talk to him 'when he'd calmed down a bit.'

He flopped down on the bed again, drew his knees up under his chin and fixed his gaze on the screen. The tall, fair-haired central defender was rising majestically to meet a long clearance from the opposition penalty area. A striker was there too, but there was never any doubt about who was going to get the ball. With a powerful flick of his head the defender directed the ball into the path of a wing back already racing up the touchline.

That's how it should be done.

Next day Owen arrived home to find a pair of new football boots on the kitchen table. Not quite top of the range, but far better than any pair he'd ever had.

He felt himself go hot as a wave of resentment swept over him. One measly trial and she gets a pair of new boots. It wasn't fair. He felt an urge to pick them up when no one was looking and chuck them in the bin. Except it wouldn't stop her playing; they'd just buy some more.

Then Jessica came clattering in wearing another pair; a pair he recognized. They were the first new ones he'd ever had; they were a tenth birthday present. He'd been so proud of them he'd worn them around the house all day.

'They're mine!' he said.

Mum laughed. 'Not much use to you now. They're far too small. They're just right for Jessica to play about in.'

Mum didn't understand, did she? And there was no point in trying to explain. He had to get out of the house.

'I'm off on a bike ride,' he said, heading for the door.

'Oh, would you take Jessica? She's been dying to go, and I don't like her going out on her own. Don't go out of the estate, will you?'

Owen said nothing, but stormed out to the garage to fetch his bike. As he wheeled it down the path, Jessica was sitting on the step pulling on her trainers.

'Wait for me!' she said.

He had no intention of waiting for anybody. He mounted his bike and rode it out of the gate, down the avenue and round the circle at the end, skidding his back wheel round. As he came back past his house, Jessica was emerging from the gate but he ignored her. He wasn't going to let her cramp his style.

He pedalled furiously up and down the streets as fast as he could go. Jessica kept appearing out of little passageways that linked the streets between some of the houses, yelling, 'Wait for me!' It would have been quite funny if he'd been in the mood.

And then, suddenly, she shot out in front of him. He tried to swerve round her, but his arms seemed locked to the handlebars. It was like somebody else was steering and he was just a helpless passenger.

It seemed like minutes as the distance between his bike and Jessica's grew less and less. He watched his front wheel hit Jessica's bike side on. He watched her fall off and the bike come down on top of her. He jumped as his own bike toppled and joined the heap in the road.

He was vaguely aware of Chris running up and pulling the bikes off Jessica's still form. No sound. Then she started whimpering and a wave of relief swept over him.

Other people arrived; eventually Mum, who took charge. She checked Jessica over.

'I don't think there's anything broken, but that ankle doesn't look too good. We'd better get you down to casualty,' she said.

Jessica's crying had turned to shuddering sobs 'I . . . I'm sorry, Mum. It was my fault. I wasn't watching where I was going.'

Was that true? Owen wasn't sure. If he hadn't been rushing around and ignoring her . . .

'You and Chris can take the bikes back home.' Mum was talking to him. 'And the Beamsley manager rang. He wants to see you play again tomorrow. It's a practice match against Hightown.'

Chris grinned. 'That's what I was coming to tell you.'

By kick-off time Owen had got over the surprise of being called back. He was feeling nervous, but excited as well. The manager had talked to him and told him to try to do more with the ball once he'd won it – little layoffs to midfield, more deliberate passes upfield rather than a hurried blast to no one in particular.

'You're good in the air,' he said. 'You win a lot more than you lose. And not many get past you once you're committed to the tackle.'

Did he mean it? The trouble was, Owen remembered the ones he missed, especially when he was punished for them. At least he now had another chance to prove himself.

Chris came over. 'You feeling OK?'

'Sort of.'

'Just don't let any weedy little striker come and knock you over, right?'

'If you don't let them sidestep you!'

Chris threw his baseball cap at him. 'How's Jessica?'

'Fed up. Her ankle's strapped and she'll be out of action for a couple of weeks or so. Could have been worse.'

Funny how things worked out. Now that she couldn't play, Owen felt quite sorry for her. He'd even promised to play with her when she got better. After all, ever since he could remember he'd wished he had a younger brother to play football with.

Meanwhile, he was going to go out there and play out of his skin. So, when Jessica did eventually don the yellow shirt of the Beamsley Beacons, people would say, 'Hey – isn't that Owen Foley's sister?'

The Boffin Bounces Back

David Harmer

When Brian Butterworth walked in through the door of Atko's classroom that first day of term, I can honestly say I had never seen anything like him. I was used to brainy kids – there was Charlotte Adams, there was Joe Stubbins – but Brian Butterworth was in a different league. When it came to brains, we were all in Division One and he was champion of the Premiership.

He even looked brainy. Big glasses, skinny legs, skinny arms, red hair all over the place, old-fashioned clothes, shoes with laces, proper grey trousers, even a tie. A tie! There hadn't been a lad in a tie at Thorpe Lane Primary for twenty-five years – not since my dad went there, and Basher Briggs was the headmaster with the longest, twitchiest cane in South Yorkshire. But Brian wore a tie, and you know what? It suited him!

That first morning, on the yard during break, we all talked about our holidays. Sean Davies went on and on about Florida, and I told my mate Dekko about Whitby. Brian came over to us.

'Look,' he said, 'let's get it sorted out right away.'

'What?' I asked.

'My nickname.'

'How about Softie Cedric?' sneered Billy Stones. We all grinned.

'Ridiculous!' snapped Brian. 'You have two choices. I'm either called Brain, a simple anagram of my name, or the Boffin. I don't mind which – you choose.'

Billy closed his open mouth. Then opened it again. 'I still think Softie Cedric's best,' he said.

Brian looked at him coolly through his enormous glasses. 'You, I take it, are the Tough Kid. Very well, here's the deal. No rough stuff and I help you with that maths Mr Atkinson set us before break, which,' and here he gazed at all of us with a smile, 'I am afraid to say was so pathetically easy that I wondered if I was in Year Six or Reception.'

'The Boffin,' said Billy firmly. 'My pal the Boffin.' And they walked off, heads together, whispering numbers.

The next day, Brian was wearing a home-made badge with *It's Cool To Be a Boffin* written on it, and he delighted us all by correcting Atko's maths.

Atko is a great teacher, really friendly and really firm. No messing with Mr Atkinson. He also runs the school football team and that makes him a bit special. I play in goal, and most games I let in just one or two less than our team scores. Some games I don't.

I think Atko was as surprised by Brian as we were.

'I'm sorry, young Butterworth,' he said, smiling, the piece of chalk rolling in his hands, 'I've done *what*?'

'Well, Mr Atkinson, you've multiplied 57 by 73 and got 4,217 when in fact the answer is 4,161.'

'Brian, did you work that out in your head just now?'

'Yes. I can do that sort of thing. My last teacher, Mr Baines, used to shout at me for doing it.'

Atko laughed. 'Really? Well I won't do that. In your head, eh?'

'Yes. And I'm sorry, Mr Atkinson, but 987 times 85 should be 83,895 not 82,908.'

Atko gave him a very funny look which, a few days later, resulted in the Boffin having special maths lessons doing very hard sums with the headteacher, Mrs Bellinger, whilst we struggled away with Mr Atkinson's easier ones.

In science he was even sharper, and none of the teachers could tell him much about computers. Nobody minded though. He couldn't help being extra clever. Like Billy Stones said, 'The Boffin's OK! It's not his fault he was born with a brain five sizes too big. Poor lad.'

Brian was really friendly too. He always helped out with work if you were stuck, and he joined in all our games on the yard.

Except, that is, when it came to football. We were still allowed on the field at dinner time as it was only September, and we had huge games between the two Year Six classes. The Boffin wouldn't play. He just stood there, all skinny and specky, looking at us as though we were just red-faced idiots lumbering around trying to kick a silly ball and falling over and arguing all the time, when in fact we were Juventus versus Manchester United.

We asked him to play but he just said, 'A ridiculous game. All that sweat and hard work for what? To kick a plastic sphere a little further over the grass and destroy the daisies. Stupid.'

Even when Vicky Rees, the most beautiful girl in the world and one of the best footballers in the universe, asked him with a smile as sweet as seven thousand sackfuls of sugar to come and have a kickabout, he just stared at the ground, went bright red and stomped off.

One evening, about five o'clock, I was cutting through the school grounds to get to Dekko's house to see if we were going down to the park. As I turned the corner by Year Six's room I saw Billy Stones flat on the ground, wriggling over the grass up the slight rise that led to the playground. Beyond Billy I could hear the thump of a football against the wall in the yard. Because of the rise, I couldn't see who was playing.

To start with I just thought it was someone who had been silly enough not to pay Billy back his gobstoppers or return his borrowed football magazines, but then I realized Billy wouldn't be snaking over the turf like a demented boa constrictor, but would be simply pummelling them into dust. So I crawled up behind him. For the first and only time in my life I made Billy Stones jump out of his skin.

The next minute I was flat on my back like a stranded kipper, and he was sitting on my chest with his fist raised. I was about to scream when he saw it was me, and relaxed.

'Lee, it's you,' he whispered.

I sat up. 'I know it is,' I whispered back. 'Billy?'

'What?'

'Why are we whispering? Who's asleep?'

'No one. Look.'

We crawled to the lip of the small hill and peered down into the yard. There was indeed a lad there, pounding the wall with a football. The boy was trapping the ball, flicking it up and catching it on his knee, flicking it over to his other knee, spinning it onto the ground and slamming it into the top corner of the wall, controlling the rebound perfectly, juggling and dancing with the ball so that it almost began to sing, then drilling it into the lowest corner of the wall and neatly trapping the return.

And that boy was Brian.

It was amazing. The skinny arms and knobbly legs were perfectly balanced, the ball responded as though by magic to his every move. He was a natural, a genius, a star.

'Boffin!' yelled Billy. 'Give us a kick?'

It was like one of those folk stories when the boy sees the elves dancing, and as soon as they see him they scatter like leaves in the wind. The Boffin took one horrified look at us, picked up his ball and ran for the gate.

He nearly made it.

'Hey Billy!' he complained. 'Put me down!'

'Sorry,' said Billy, doing just that. 'I got carried away.'

I helped Brian up again. 'That was fantastic. You're brilliant!'

'Of course I am,' he said. 'What a pity it's such a stupid game.'

'What?' said Billy.

'I'm sorry, guys, I should have told you, I suppose. It's not that I can't play football, it's just that I don't want to. I can't stand the game. Sorry.'

'How can you be so good at football and never play it?' I asked, feeling totally bewildered.

'I don't mind a bit of fun with the ball,' Brian explained. 'I quite like that. It's having to be in a team with everybody shouting and teachers getting cross and all that. Mr Baines went crazy if I didn't play well. So, I've decided to pack it in.' He looked at us quite fiercely. 'Sometimes being good at everything isn't such a laugh.'

'Come on, eh?' said Billy. 'Let's have a kickabout.'

At first Brian wouldn't join in, but we said, 'Oh, go on, Boff' enough times to persuade him. Once he started, he dazzled us with his skill. He was even beginning to look like he was enjoying things. My cousin Darren turned up on his bike and soon we were having a decent game. He's a bit goofy, our Darren, but he's a nice enough lad. We played for about half an hour and then it was time to go home for tea.

The next day the story was all over school. Even Atko heard about it.

'I'm told, young Butterworth,' he said just before we went off to assembly, 'that you are a bit of a whiz with a football. Why not join the team?'

'Yeah, go on, Boffin,' said Billy. 'You were really something with that ball.'

'The statistical chances of getting permanent damage in the leg, knee, ankle and brain from playing football are too high, unlike chess or billiards. So I prefer not to join in,' said Brian. 'Besides, you get all muddy and cold and people yell at you very rudely. I don't know what you see in it.'

We knew him by now. Lots of big words, but was it all a wind-up?

'Oh, go on, Bri,' I said. 'The school team needs some good players.'

'That's right,' agreed Atko. 'Our demon winger, Ben Todd, has moved to Scarborough. After Lee here, he was our leading goalscorer.'

They all laughed. Honestly, one own-goal and a few I let in by accident and everyone's a comedian.

'If you have a cricket team in the summer, Mr Atkinson, I will be scorer, but that's it. Sorry.'

'OK, Brian, but until Ben left we had a strong chance in the Inter-Schools Cup. We play each year and usually do quite well. This year we've actually made the semi-final. I'm afraid losing Ben gives us a real problem. Perhaps you're the lad we need to solve it.'

Brian said nothing, just looked rather embarrassed and made his glasses slide up and down his nose by wrinkling his forehead.

'Mr Atkinson, I don't mean to be rude, but what is the point of football?'

'Er . . . to have fun, to win.'

The Boffin looked at him very seriously. 'There's more fun to be had in mathematics than football. It seems to me a game for simpletons.'

There was a bit of an awkward pause. Atko rubbed his chin thoughtfully.

'Fair enough, Brian. I shan't nag any more.'

We did though. We nagged him like crazy. Unlike Atko, we'd seen him kick a football. We knew that Brian could make a football walk, talk and do the dishes. We made sure he was nagged all right.

By the end of the dinner-break he was weakening. By afternoon break he'd agreed to think about it just to shut us up. Then, just before the bell, Dekko was chasing Joanne Webster in a game of tiggy, tripped over his shoelace and came crashing down onto the tarmac.

Dekko's yelp of pain was loud and real enough to make us all stop and stare. Atko was on duty and he ran over straightaway. Mrs Bellinger came out and, with Atko's help, they got Dekko inside school. It looked nasty and, after break, Atko told us the grim news.

'I thought everyone should know that Gary Dexter has severely twisted his ankle. And I heard this morning that we are down to play Town End Juniors in the semi-final next Tuesday. It looks a bit tough, lads. I know we'll all do our best, but we are now short of two of our best players.'

That was it – no striker. No slinky, sneaky, slippy little goalscorer to match Billy's big battle charges up the front end. Dekko was out of the game for weeks.

Worse, we were playing against Town End, the school on the other side of the estate, our rivals in everything. They were always a good side and really hard to beat. Worse still, our Darren played in their midfield. Losing to them meant weeks of his goofy laugh and even goofier insults.

We would give it a good shot, but it was hard to see how we'd win without Dekko and Ben. We'd lost our last game six–two. Before that it had been two–two, and before that we'd won five–four.

And here we were with a match-winning genius who wouldn't play. Brilliant.

We nagged some more. Eventually, once we'd explained the position and how important it was to defeat the Town Enders, Brian agreed to meet us in the park on Saturday to have a practice game.

'I promise nothing,' he said, 'but I can see you are in a tight spot, so just this once I'll give it a go.'

It rained most of Saturday morning, but by the afternoon it was sunny again. It's never serious down the park. We just put together some teams of boys and girls from at least three or four different schools and it's usually really good fun. There's always some Town Enders there including, on this occasion, my cousin.

'You've got us then.' Darren smiled a toothy smile.

'Yeah.'

'I heard Ben and Dekko are out of the game.'

'Yeah.'

'Come on, Lee,' said Darren. 'Admit it, you're going to lose!'

'We'll whip you daft!' I shouted, half joking, half angry. 'You'll see.'

'OK,' said Darren, holding his hands palm outwards. 'Just cool it.'

We picked teams, about fifteen a side, and started.

The Boffin turned up, in tracksuit and T-shirt, looking weedy and skinny and about as much like a footballer as my baby brother Carl.

'New kid!' I yelled. 'We'll have him.'

A big lad on their team sized Brian up. 'You can keep him,' he laughed. 'Looks a bit of a nerd to me.'

Darren, who knew better, pulled a face but it was too late. The Boffin was on the pitch, studying the opposition. It looked like he was working out the statistical chances of scoring a goal against fifteen players, five of them goalies, and calculating the angle at which to run at the packed defence so as to cut through it. I never discovered what would have happened, because the moment he joined the game, Dean Webb and Danny Hobson did as well.

I groaned. It could only mean trouble. They were both Town Enders, really good players but nasty with it. In a school game they were tamed by teachers. In the park on a Saturday afternoon, it would be a different story.

'We're playing now,' grunted Danny. 'Right?'

'Any Thorpe Laneites can get on the other side so we can practise murdering you,' ordered Dean. 'Like we will in the semi-final.'

We rearranged the teams and Dean and Danny kicked off.

Then they saw the Boffin. The game stopped.

'What is *that*?' yelled Dean.

'It's a matchstick man,' shouted Danny. 'Skinny body, red head.'

'Now then, matchstick man, don't snap in half, eh?'

'Yeah, don't go on strike.'

They kept this up until Vicky Rees restarted the game by scoring a goal. There was an immediate argument as the other team said they hadn't been ready.

All this time the Boffin hadn't moved. I ran over.

'You OK, Bri?' I asked.

'Eh?' He seemed in a dream. 'Oh, you mean the apes? Don't worry, Lee, I'm used to all that.'

'Bri, they've stopped arguing. Let's go, huh?'

'Apemen always call me names,' he grinned. 'But one day I will be earning thousands and they will still be apemen, right?'

With that he sprinted off, slid the ball away from Dean's toe, skipped over a lunge from Danny, somehow wriggled past seven more players and four of the goalies and would have scored – but he was badly fouled and landed head down in one of the muddiest puddles in the park.

'Sorry, stick insect!' hooted Dean. 'My leg slipped. Honest!'

'Oh dear,' said Danny, rubbing the Boffin's face with

his muddy hands so that all you could see were a pair of gleaming circles where his glasses were. 'Matchstick man seems to have got stuck.'

'A stuck stick,' said Dean. 'Let's unstick him.'

Before anyone could protest or say anything, poor old Brian had been scooped out of the mud by the pair of them and dropped into an enormous puddle just by the edge of our pitch.

'That's put his spark out a bit,' laughed Dean.

My heart sank. Brian was soaking and even his cool had cracked. He got up, waded out of the puddle and, muttering Boffin-like bad things under his breath, stormed off home. Our plans to bring him into the team were wrecked.

Nobody saw Brian that weekend but on Monday we were waiting in the yard before school began, knowing what he would say and hoping to change his mind. The semi-final was after school the following evening. We needed him.

It was useless.

'If you think I am playing those clowns again,' he said, 'to be treated like that, I'm not. Besides,' and he sneezed loudly, 'after that drenching, I've caught a cold. I'm not fit to play.'

'It'll be different, Brian,' I told him. 'We'll have a referee. They listen to teachers, you know.'

'Yeah,' agreed Vicky, 'it's well known, they're on a final warning. Any more rough stuff and they get dropped for three weeks.'

'Forget it. Those two dumbos make me sick.' He sneezed once more. 'Sick in more ways than one.'

'I'll help you out,' said Billy. 'They don't bother me much.'

'No, Billy,' I said. 'Remember the last game?'

'Oh yeah.'

'What?' asked Brian.

'Dean and Danny needled Billy all through the first ten minutes. Kicked his ankles, pulled his shirt, whispered names at him. The ref saw nothing.'

'I got really mad at them,' admitted Billy. 'Lost my head a bit.'

'And got sent off,' I said. 'It was a set-up, you see. They did it on purpose to weaken our attack. Of course we lost.'

Suddenly, something deep inside my head began to buzz and glow like the bars of my grandad's electric fire, turning a dull crimson and slowly getting brighter until it clicked into red-hot light.

'Billy,' I said. 'The night we saw the Boff play in the school yard, the night we discovered his genius ... Think, Bill, think. Who was there?'

Billy looked at me. 'What are you on about, Lee?' he said. 'Your Darren was there, all the time!'

His face lost its clouded look and he began to smile. 'Of course! It was before the cup draw – it didn't matter what he knew then, did it?'

I turned and grabbed Brian by his coat. 'Brian, that stuff in the park, it was a set-up.'

I turned to face all of them, September sun in my face, Mrs Bellinger just about to ring the bell, everything in slow motion. 'They set out to get you, Brian. They wanted to scare you off, frighten you out of playing. You've been nobbled.'

'How did they know he'd be at the park?' asked Billy.

'They just guessed. If it hadn't have been then, they would have pulled the same stunt another time.'

Brian's intelligence gleamed out of his eyes like a searchlight. 'Lee,' he said, 'you're right. It is a set-up. And I'll tell you what, no apeman is going to push me out of anything. I'll play!'

Our cheers stopped short as a violent sneezing fit attacked him. He looked up from behind his soggy tissues.

'Don't know how I'll get through a whole match, though,' he said.

The next night after school we lined up against Town End Primary. Billy was up at the front with Sean Davis instead of Dekko. Sean was solid enough and usually played midfield, but today was a different game. Joe Stubbins was on the wing for Ben, but we had a makeshift air about us. Atko had been very keen on playing Brian at once, but Brian had said he wasn't fit enough for a whole game. Atko, of course, did not know that we had a plan.

'I'm too skinny,' Brian explained to our patient teacher, 'and I have a bad cold. So, my body weight multiplied by the energy I shall use, divided by the time factor . . .'

'Yes, yes, Brian,' Atko said. 'You can come on as substitute.'

On the field, Atko was a bit puzzled because he couldn't see Brian anywhere. We didn't explain and, before he could ask any awkward questions, we kicked off. Straight away we were up against it. Ben on the wing was badly missed and however hard Sean and Joe tried, they couldn't make an impression. Most of the first fifteen minutes were spent defending, with me pulling off three saves, one of which, though I say so myself, was pretty spectacular.

'You wait, Lee!' Dean Webb grunted as I tipped his second deadly shot over the bar. 'We're going to get a bucketful today.'

Then they took a quick goal kick and, after four swift passes, Dean Webb swept the ball past me and into the goal.

'Like I said, Lee,' he sneered, 'the first of many!'

'Pity stick man was too scared to join us,' laughed Danny.

'Not much good as striker, was he?' said Dean. 'Too wet.'

Two minutes later, our Darren nearly scored.

'Traitor,' I muttered. He goofed at me with his cheesy grin.

'All's fair in football, Lee,' he said. 'Sorry.'

The game was fierce in the midfield, with the ball going backwards and forwards between the two teams, but Dean and Danny were very strong. It wasn't too long before three more had blazed past me. I could see it was going to be one of those days.

Then Billy's fourth or fifth brave charge at their defence ended up with the ball bobbling about in the Town Enders' area, and Sean poked out a toe and scored.

At half-time it was four–one. Atko's team talk was great. He looked worried sick but he was full of praise.

'Keep trying, lads,' he said. 'That last goal was full of guts and determination. Well played, Billy and Sean. We can still do it. Lee, hang in there, son. Remember, a goalie is as good as his defence. We just need goals.' His face fell. 'I'm sorry, but Brian has let us down badly. I can't find him anywhere. Go for it, lads. You can win.'

We knew he was trying his best. We also knew that

with this line-up we couldn't win. However, unlike poor Atko, we knew just where Brian was.

After a few more minutes of scrapping for every ball and fighting every challenge, the Enders got a throw-on. Suddenly Joe Stubbins shot off the pitch shouting, 'Sub, Mr Atkinson! Now, please.'

Atko, rather bewildered, shouted, 'Sub, ref.'

The ref nodded his agreement and one of the bushes near the edge of the pitch sneezed loudly. The Boffin emerged from hiding and raced onto the field.

As superheroes go he wasn't much to look at. He wasn't any stronger looking, his legs weren't any thicker, his specs were as round and as gleaming as ever, and he was obviously full of cold. But the effect on the Town Enders was amazing. Dean gasped, Danny said, 'What?' and their throw was wasted and fell right at my feet. I whacked it upfield and, in his first touch, Brian took the ball with his back to their goal and whipped it over his head into the roof of the net. The crowd was silent as we yelled and whooped.

'Lucky old stick man,' jibed Dean.

'Mathematics,' he replied. 'Distance and estimated wind power. Easy.'

That was four–two. There was still a battle to fight, but now our team was recharged. Our back four tackled like mad and our midfield were inspired. Suddenly, Brian was right in the heaving mass of feet and elbows. He danced out, the ball glued to his feet. As Dean and Danny both came crunching in to sandwich him, the Boffin flicked the ball over their heads, jumped over their legs, left them sprawling in the mud and tapped in the third.

Atko was jumping up and down. 'Ten minutes left, lads,' he yelled. 'Go for it!'

Brian had the ball again. He dropped his shoulder, jinked and jived through three tackles and slipped the ball past our Darren, wiping that goofy smile right off his face. Brian whipped round the full back, pulled their goalie off his line and ran round him. Four all.

In those last minutes, Dean and Danny were like charging bulls. They came after Brian with murder in their eyes. It did no good. They gave away three free-kicks and Brian curled a mathematically perfect goal in from every one. As the game drew to its close, he faced them both one last time, sneezed, pulled the ball onto his left foot, scooped it in the air, juggled it twice on his knee, nipped in between them, and then slammed it in the goal. He turned round to discover Dean and Danny sitting in the mud just behind him, back to back, their heads spinning.

The whistle went and we had won eight–four. We were through to the final, for the first time ever in the history of the school.

Just before we left for home, Mrs Bellinger came over to us and said, 'Brian, that was remarkable. The question is, will you play in the final?'

He pursed his lips, dabbed his nose and wiped his eyes. 'The statistical chance of me doing that,' he began, and we all groaned, 'is a one hundred per cent certainty. You bet I'll play.'

We cheered, and Billy shouted, 'Now we'll flipping win!'

And we flipping did.

The Twitcher

Redvers Brandling

'*Aaaaaagh!*'

The sharp cry of pain cut through the frosty air like a dry branch snapping. It was followed by a piercing blast from the referee's whistle. The pile of bodies in the goal mouth began to disentangle themselves.

Red and white shirts pulled away from others in dark blue, but the green-clad goalie lay still on the bone-hard pitch.

'It's Jamie!' cried Ollie Martin, manager of Waltham Under-13s. 'Come on.'

Harry Morley – the Waltham captain, not playing today because of a heavy cold – raced onto the pitch with Ollie. As he did so, thoughts whirled through his head. Jamie Bywaters was the best keeper for miles around. Today's game was just a league match, but next Saturday morning it was the district cup final, and if Jamie . . .

'Doesn't look good,' sighed the ref, as Ollie and Harry reached the goal mouth.

'Let's have a look, sunshine,' said Ollie in his kindly way.

Jamie's face was almost as green as his sweater as he held his right elbow in his left hand, and showed a rapidly swelling right wrist.

'Ah – a bad sprain that is,' said Ollie briskly. As a

nurse he knew what he was talking about. 'No more football for you for a bit. Off we go then.'

Between them, Ollie and Harry helped Jamie off the pitch. Jamie's dad was amongst the spectators, so Jamie was off to the doctor's in a flash.

'Howard!' called Ollie, as Jamie and his dad left. 'Substitute goalie – get on there.'

'Pardon?' answered Howard Simpson's dreamy voice.

'On – on – on – get on there!'

'Oh, right.'

Harry groaned to himself. One of Howard Simpson's boots was untied, and his goalie's jersey was on back to front. He'd been gazing at the sky when Ollie called him – miles away, as usual.

Minutes later, the match was on again. At the time of Jamie's injury, Waltham were three–nil up with only twenty minutes to go – nothing to worry about. But their goalkeeper's injury had unsettled the team and Enford, their opponents, sensed that all was not now lost. They surged into attack.

'Back, Billy!' shouted their hefty striker as the marauding right back swept up to the bye line.

Elliott Bell, Waltham's best defender, had dealt with dozens of situations like this. As the ball came in he took it calmly on his chest, calling, 'Yours, Howard.'

It was an easy, and obvious, goalie's ball, but Howard was far too slow to come for it. In a flash, the Enford striker's foot smashed into the ball.

Waltham 3 Enford 1.

As the players ran back to the centre circle, Elliott gave Howard one of his blackest looks.

'Wake up, Simmo – *concentrate*, man!'

'Sorry, Elliott,' replied Howard, holding up a hand. 'I'll be OK now.'

Having got one goal back, Enford were now full of confidence. Attack after attack poured down on the Waltham defence, and Elliott, with the rest of the back four and all the midfielders, were just about overrun.

Shots rained in on Howard, but now he was like a man inspired. Punching, diving, flicking over the bar, blocking with his body, he let nothing past him.

Biting his lip, Harry shuffled restlessly on the touchline.

'We're going to do it, Ollie, we're going to get the points.'

'Yeah,' agreed the manager, looking at his watch.

Some of the steam had gone out of Enford now and the ball was back with their goalkeeper. Forlornly, but with a mighty kick nevertheless, he booted it upfield. His tired forwards watched as the ball sailed over their heads, and the Waltham defenders smiled contentedly. An easy ball for the goalie . . .

But Howard wasn't even watching!

Gazing at some distant movement in the far-off marshes he was only aware of the ball as it sailed past him and rippled down the back of the net.

'I don't . . .' began Ollie desperately.

'I do,' sighed Harry.

But the sharp blast of the referee's whistle ending the match stopped further conversation.

The team met again on the following Tuesday night for their weekly session in Oldfield School hall. They used this time for practice and chatting about the last game – and the next one.

'Jamie's out for six weeks,' was the first thing Ollie said to Harry when he arrived.

'I thought he might be,' replied the skipper. 'What are we going to do about a goalie for Saturday?'

'Let's talk about it after the practice,' puffed Ollie, running on the spot as fast as he could. 'The other lads are coming in now and we don't want to waste any time.'

Oldfield hall was big, and five-a-side matches offered good competitive practice. Ollie always played for a full hour in these sessions – and it was obvious how near he must once have been to being full professional standard.

Tonight he kept changing the players around – with one exception. He kept Howard Simpson permanently in goal and against what was always the stronger team – the one he himself was playing for.

'Come on! Come on!' yelled Ollie. 'We've had all the play and we're still not winning!'

Harry, who was playing behind Ollie, nodded his head and muttered under his breath. 'Typical,' he sighed, 'absolutely flippin' typical.'

What was typical, of course, was Howard's performance in goal. Playing indoors there were no passing birds or distant bird songs to distract him. He was all attention – and he was good.

Let's just see how good, thought Harry.

Taking a rolled pass from Elliott Bell, Harry suddenly accelerated down the middle of the hall. Brushing two tackles aside he feinted to hit the ball with his right foot – and then brought his left leg through to hit a screamer about a foot from the floor.

Never taking his eyes off Harry's feet and the ball, Howard didn't even flicker as Harry's feint tempted a sudden move. But when the shot came hurtling in, he was down like a panther, with the ball cradled in his arms.

'Great stop, How!' called Ollie, and then gave a long blast on his whistle. 'That's it, lads. Showers quick and then on your way.'

Half an hour later, Harry sat in Ollie's car as the manager drummed his fingers on the steering wheel.

'Team picks itself for Saturday, don't you think?'

Harry pulled an ear with thumb and forefinger. 'Up to a point – but what about Simpson?'

'Well, you saw him tonight – he was great.'

'In there he was great, but you know what he's like outside. A couple of sparrows fly over and he's just about airborne himself.'

Ollie punched Harry lightly on the shoulder. 'You're exaggerating. I know he's a mad-keen bird watcher – they call them "twitchers", you know – but even with a twitcher in goal on Saturday we'll win.'

'Hmmm. I hope you're right. I'll go and see him on Friday night after he's got your letter telling him he's in the team.'

There was just about an hour of daylight left when Harry left school on Friday. He knew where Howard would be.

Usual place, thought Harry to himself. *Low Valley bird hide, with binoculars glued to his eyes.*

Sure enough, when the Waltham skipper pushed open the squeaky door of the wooden bird hide, there was one person in it – Howard.

'Hi.'

Howard heard Harry's greeting but didn't turn from the observation slit.

'Hi,' he muttered absently, never taking the binoculars from his eyes.

'What are you looking at?' asked Harry.

'A heron. It's a beauty – what a flight!'

'Howard, I've come to talk to you about Saturday's match.'

Howard lowered his binoculars and turned round.

'Oh, it's you, Harry – yeah OK – I'll be just a minute . . . I'll just watch . . .'

Harry sighed as Howard turned back to the slit.

'No, Howard, we've got to talk . . .'

Suddenly he was cut off by a strangled yell from Howard.

'I don't believe it! Why the . . .'

'What is it?' gasped Harry in surprise.

'He's still doing it . . . a hit could kill her! Come on!'

Dropping his binoculars, Howard turned and dashed for the door. An amazed Harry followed him.

'But what is it?' panted Harry again as the two boys pelted along the gravel path beside the lake.

'A thug – hurling half bricks at an old coot near the nests.'

A minute later, the two boys stood gaping at a flattened spot on the water's edge.

'Gone!' muttered Howard bitterly. 'But I tell you what, Harry – I got a good look at him through the binoculars. Already running then he was – but I'd recognize him again anywhere.'

'Right,' agreed Harry. 'It was a rotten thing to do.'

As the boys walked back to the hide, Harry gradually brought the conversation back to Saturday's match, but after a while he gave up. He knew he wasn't getting through to his angry companion.

*

The morning of the district cup final dawned bright and clear. It was so chilly you could see your breath steaming in the air and the pale blue sky was empty of clouds.

Hmm – I expect he could see a bird five miles away today! Harry thought apprehensively as he dropped his bag of kit on the floor.

This was a special match in more ways than one. For a start, Hildesdon Town were letting it take place on their pitch. They were a well-set-up non-league club with dressing rooms, a grandstand, floodlights – the lot.

'This is the stuff, lads, isn't it?' enthused an excited Ollie, rubbing his hands together vigorously. 'Just like the old days when I used to play.'

'Oh you mean back with the dinosaurs,' chuckled Elliott cheekily.

'That'll do from you,' snapped Ollie, clapping his hands and running on the spot. 'Now listen,' he said sharply, suddenly standing quite still and getting their attention. 'I've been doing my homework on this team we're playing – and they're good. Good – but not unbeatable. They've got two stars, a ginger-haired mid-fielder who is a super passer, and a real livewire of a centre forward. Now watch out for this last bloke in particular. He doesn't look anything – a thin lad with bright blond hair – but he's mustard. Harry, you're going to have to watch him like a hawk, and Howard, be careful because he's always trying tricky shots.'

'OK, Ollie,' replied Harry. 'Got that, Howard?'

'Oh . . . er yes, Harry, I mean Ollie . . . yes.' A startled Howard looked up from a book on bird recognition he was reading in the corner of the dressing room.

'Heaven help us,' muttered Harry to himself.

The next five minutes were spent limbering up, rubbing legs and making nervous jokes. Then the dressing room door opened and the referee looked in.

'OK, lads, off we go,' he said. 'Let's have a good game.'

Harry picked up a ball and, with a clattering of boots, the rest of the team followed him up the corridor to the patch of daylight at the end.

'WALTHAM ... WALTHAM ... WALTHAM!' chanted the fans as Harry and the boys ran out onto the pitch.

It was an impressive sight. There were hundreds in the grandstand and round the touchline, and the red and white colours contrasted with the old gold of the opposition.

'BARCLAY ... BARCLAY ... BARCLAY!' A second chant broke out as the Barclay Rovers team ran onto the pitch.

Looking good in their Wolverhampton Wanderers type old-gold strip, they raced to the far end of the ground.

'They look like Wolves, but can they play like them?' shouted Elliott to Micky Deacon, one of the midfielders.

'We'll soon find out!'

By now the Waltham lads were kicking in at Howard, who was casually fielding the half-hit shots. Harry was keeping an eye open for the referee's signal when suddenly Howard left his goal and raced towards him.

What now? thought Harry as the goalkeeper reached him and grabbed his arm with a grip like iron.

'What . . .?' began the skipper.

'It's *him*, Harry! I'd know him anywhere. It's him, I tell you!'

'Hang on, Howard. What are you talking about?'

'It's him – the lout who was hurling those bricks at the coots down on the lake.'

Howard pointed a gloved finger at the slight blond figure in old gold at the other end. The black number 9 stood out starkly on his back as he headed goalward.

'There's no doubt about it – it's him.'

Before Harry could reply, the restless figure of the referee, waving his arms and blowing his whistle, summoned the two captains to the centre circle. Leaving the motionless Howard still staring at the other end, the skipper ran off.

With a grin the Barclay captain shook hands and, at the ref's invitation, called heads as the coin was flung into the air.

'Heads it is,' said the ref.

'Not much wind about,' muttered the Barclay captain, 'so we might as well stay as we are.'

The first ten minutes of the match were a cautious affair. Both teams were feeling each other out, and nobody wanted to make any mistakes. The match was too important. Twice Harry got the ball in his own half with nobody near him. Each time he turned and passed the ball back to Howard to give the goalie an early feel of the ball.

'Howard!' he called each time in a loud voice. But he needn't have worried. Howard was alert, with the most intense look of concentration on his face that Harry had ever seen. Each time, Howard collected the ball and booted it upfield without a word.

It was in the twelfth minute that the match suddenly came devastatingly to life.

Elliott Bell cracked a low, skimming pass out into space on the right wing. Charlie Jackson, the Waltham right winger, immediately set off after it at full speed. The Barclay left back went with him, and the two players were neck and neck as they reached the ball. There was a blur of old gold as the defender flung himself into a sliding tackle – but he wasn't quick enough. At the last second, Charlie tapped the ball beyond the defender's outstretched foot and, as the Barclay man lay gasping on the ground, he sped goalwards. Shouts came from the penalty area.

'Now, Charlie, now!' called Elroy Jess, the Waltham striker.

'Cover the back post!' shrieked the alarmed goalkeeper.

'WALTHAM!' cried the crowd at this first serious attack.

Charlie ignored everything but the ball at his feet. As he neared the meeting of the penalty area with the bye line he made as if to cross with his right foot. In anticipation, the goalie immediately lunged out to catch the centre he thought was coming. As he did so, Charlie cut out from the bye line and hit a vicious left-foot shot from a narrow angle.

It rocketed goalwards, hit the underside of the bar and flew into the far corner of the net.

Waltham 1 Barclay 0.

'WALTHAM – THE GREATEST!' shouted the red and white supporters.

'Fantastic goal, Charlie!' congratulated Harry as he slapped the winger on the back and the rest of the team crowded round the delighted scorer. 'How about another like it?'

But the goal stung Barclay into quick retaliation. It

was now that the two stars Ollie had warned the Waltham team about came into their own. The ball seemed to move to the ginger-haired midfielder as if drawn by a magnet. Once he had it, Ginger probed the Waltham defence with a mixture of long and short passes, flicks, chips and lobs.

'Go, Bobby, go!' he yelled as he directed anything and everything in the direction of the thin blond striker.

Harry soon realized just how good Bobby was. The centre forward could control the ball with either foot, and he was full of clever tricks. It took all Harry's concentration to try and mark him tightly.

After about ten minutes of intense Barclay pressure, Ginger suddenly burst through on the left.

'Now, Bobby!' he shouted, this time crossing a high fast ball.

Too high for him, thought Harry, as he prepared to leap.

But it wasn't. Bobby was airborne before Harry's feet even left the ground. His forehead hit the ball with a solid thwack, and the Barclay fans were already shouting for a goal – when Howard intervened.

Flinging himself up to his left, and turning in mid-air, he managed to get a fingertip to the flying ball. It was just enough. Deflected onto the top of the bar, the ball shot off into the crowd.

Corner!

'Great save, Howard!' shouted Ollie from the touch-line, as the fans of both sides clapped.

'Terrific, Simmo,' said Elliott, giving Howard a punch on the arm.

'Well done, goalie,' muttered the blond opposition striker. 'Some save.'

Harry was too breathless to speak, but he noticed how Howard ignored the striker's comment. Then, when they were milling about before the corner kick, the goalie whispered fiercely to him, 'Don't let him score, Harry!'

But before Harry could respond, the corner came swinging across. It was hit really hard and sailed over the crowded goalmouth to the right winger, who was waiting for it. Controlling the ball in an instant he crossed it low and hard into the back of the penalty area. Like lightning Bobby raced towards it – and stepped over the speeding ball!

Behind him Ginger was waiting for just such a move. He hit the ball first time and before Howard – or anybody else for that matter – could move, there it was nestling in the back of the net.

Waltham 1 Barclay 1.

From this point until half-time, the match swung from one end of the pitch to the other. It was now being played at a terrific pace, and with lots of skill as well. But when the ref blew for half-time it was still one–all.

'You've done really well,' said Ollie quietly, when everybody was sitting in the dressing room. 'A good match and two great goals. So – how are we going to win?'

'Score more goals than them,' quipped the ever witty Elliott.

'Stop Ginger and that striker getting so much of the ball,' offered Harry as the laughter died down.

'Exactly!' snapped Ollie, pointing a finger at Harry to emphasize the point. 'So, Elliott, you move in a bit to cover Harry, and you, Micky, try and get nearer to Ginger so you can stop some of those passes.'

Without another word, Ollie went round filling up the mugs of orange squash. Then they heard the ref calling them onto the field.

The second half started like the first, with both teams sparring at each other. Everything was a bit aimless as the ball bounced around in the middle of the pitch. Then one of Ollie's tactical moves paid off. A Barclay pass from the back swept out towards Ginger, but Micky Deacon, who was now marking the midfielder much more closely, got to it first.

'Charlie!' he shouted, and lofted the ball out to the right wing. The Barclay defence were caught off guard by losing possession so quickly. Charlie Jackson was onto the ball in a flash.

This time he ignored the wing route and cut inside. Heading straight for the centre of the goal he built up a terrific speed. Off balance, the left back was left floundering behind, and the two centre backs hesitated before committing themselves. By then it was too late.

Hardly pausing in his run, Charlie hit a right-foot shot which took off from the ground like a jet fighter. The goalie saw it coming but he had no hope of reaching it as the ball rose majestically and crackled into the top corner of the net.

'What a goal!'
'Great shot, Charlie!'
'WALTHAM!'

The crowd roared as the excited Waltham team surrounded Charlie again. He would never forget this match!

But Barclay were a good team too, and for the second time in the match they went all out for the equalizer. Try as they might, Waltham were forced further and further back, until they could barely get the ball out of their own half. Yet, despite the pressure, they never looked like cracking. Harry and Elliott were magnificent at the back, and Howard saved everything that got through with supreme confidence.

'Keep it up, Harry!' shouted Ollie from the line, holding up a hand with five fingers outstretched.

'Five minutes to go – we've got to do it,' muttered Harry through gritted teeth.

One . . . two . . . three minutes went by.

With a brisk wave of his hand, Ginger waved the rear of the Barclay team to come forward. One last chance.

What happened next was a fast-moving jumble of events which climaxed in the Waltham penalty area. Ginger got the ball in midfield and, brushing Micky Deacon aside, he set off towards the Waltham goal. Elliott Bell, seeing the danger, rushed forward to meet him. When Ginger lobbed the ball goalwards, it was a straightforward race between Harry and Bobby, the striker, to see who got to it first.

As he raced for the ball, Harry was suddenly aware of a flock of gulls swooping in the sky overhead.

'Don't look at them, Howard!'

The thought flashed through his mind. But the determined Howard was already running out to collect the ball with total concentration on his face. For Harry, however, the momentary distraction was disastrous. Clumsily his right foot crashed into Bobby's racing legs, and the striker tumbled painfully in the penalty area.

The ball was safely in Howard's hands, but the referee's whistle had already gone. He pointed to the spot. Penalty!

'Sorry, lads,' muttered a shocked Harry as the Waltham team moved out of the penalty area.

'What about it, Bobby?' asked Ginger, as he helped his team-mate to his feet.

'I'm OK. Do you want me to take it?'

'Yeah, go on.'

The ball was put on the penalty spot. The crowd was silent. The ref's whistle shrilled, and Bobby ran forward.

'Thwack!'

He hit the ball crisply with the inside of his right foot, and it hurtled towards the left-hand corner of the goal. The perfect penalty. But Howard's anticipation was equal to it. With an incredible dive he just managed to get a hand to the ball. It was enough. The deflected shot skidded past the left post.

What happened next was the equal of all that had gone before. The final whistle went, the Waltham supporters roared and the Barclay fans clapped. The Barclay team, as sporting as their fans, shook hands with their opponents, but in the Waltham goal a different drama was taking place.

· The blond Barclay striker, friendly to the end, advanced on Howard Simpson with outstretched hand.

'Fantastic save, goalie! That deserved to win any match.'

To the boy's astonishment, Howard knocked his hand aside and began an angry reply.

Running towards the goal, Harry saw the two players exchange a torrent of words – and then an amazing change came over Howard's angry face.

Howard turned excitedly to him. 'Harry!' spluttered the goalkeeper. 'Bobby wasn't running away after stoning the coots – he was chasing the kid who he had seen throwing the stones. I was wrong all the time. Bobby here's a member of the Boxley Twitchers' club and . . .'

'Oh, come and get your medals,' replied Harry with a grin as wide as the goal mouth.

'Medals? . . . Oh yes . . .' muttered Howard, putting his arm around the striker's shoulders. 'Now listen, Bobby. Next Friday at the Low Valley hide . . .'

'Twitchers!' grinned Harry, shaking his head as he ran back to the centre circle. 'Mad, totally mad!'

Much Ado About Nothing

Mick Gowar

Warwickshire, 1577

Will sat up, spitting gobbets of leaf mulch and mud
out of his mouth. Above him, his older cousin Dickon
shrieked with laughter.

'You're hopeless, Will! Utterly hopeless! A simple
chase, and look at the state of you! Your doublet's all
covered in mud, and there are great holes in your
hose!'

Dickon laughed again. It was a harsh, mocking
laugh; a whining mirthless, grating laugh. It set Will's
teeth on edge, like the noise of fingernails being slowly
scraped down one of the schoolroom slates that he
and Dickon wrote on during weekdays.

Will clambered to his feet as quickly as his bruises
would allow. He hoped that his vigour might suggest
that lying face down in muck was nothing to be
ashamed of.

The two boys were standing in the middle of a
long, narrow field which was enclosed by thick thorn
hedges. At the far end, two long-legged, rough-coated
dogs scratched at the base of the hedge and whimpered
with frustration.

'Did they catch it – did they catch the hare?' Will
asked eagerly.

'No,' Dickon groaned. 'Tom managed to start a hare, but he didn't give me enough time to slip the leashes.' He held out two leather straps. Then he laced two fingers into his mouth and blew a sharp, high-pitched whistle.

The two dogs stopped sniffing and scraping at the hedge and came bounding back. They frolicked and danced around the two boys, their long pink tongues lolling and licking.

'Down!' bellowed Dickon. He lashed out with the leather leashes. The two dogs cringed and backed away. Will wanted to tell the older boy to stop; to let the dogs be excited if they wanted to be. After all, what harm were they doing?

Will heard a shout and turned round. From the opposite direction, a lanky, thin-faced boy came loping up. It was Tom, Will's father's apprentice.

'What happened?' he demanded. 'I beat a hare out of the far hedge – at the cost of a good scratching' – he held out his arm to show several scarlet weals – 'and were all my efforts in vain? Where's the hare that I clambered through briars and thorns to scare your way?'

'A poor show, Tom,' said Dickon haughtily, as if speaking to a young child or a servant. 'A very poor show. You gave me no time, no time at all! Now, go back and try again.'

The thin boy looked back at Dickon with loathing. 'Perhaps my lord high and mighty would care to show us how himself!' Tom gave a sarcastic bow.

'Don't you come the cheeky knave with me!' snarled Dickon. 'You forget who you're speaking to!' He paused to flick an imaginary speck of dust from a sleeve every bit as worn and grimy as Tom's.

'Remember you are merely Will's father's apprentice, while I am the son of the squire . . .'

'Squire?' shouted Tom. '*Squire?* Your father may call himself *Esquire* and send his son to the grammar school, but everyone in Stratford knows that your father is no more a squire than . . . than . . . than . . .' He stared around, then pointed furiously into the next field. 'Why, he's no more a squire than yonder cow's bum is!'

With a howl of rage Dickon sprang at Tom and grabbed him round the throat. Tom grabbed two handfuls of Dickon's hair, and the two boys collapsed onto the ground, kicking and gouging and struggling.

'Stop! Stop!' shouted Will, his voice shrill with panic. He couldn't bear fighting, or shouting, or disorder of any kind. 'Stop! Please, stop!' He tried to drag Dickon off, but as he pulled at Dickon's shoulder, Tom's right arm lashed out. With a yelp, Will staggered back, blood trickling from his lower lip.

Dickon gave a sudden, high-pitched shriek and let go of Tom, who rolled sideways and clambered to his feet. Dickon continued to roll on his back on the short wet grass, whimpering, gasping and holding himself with both hands.

Tom stood over the sobbing Dickon, fists bunched up. 'Come my lord! What, Sir Knight? Is your lordship defeated by a mere apprentice?' He spat out the words with real hatred.

'Low blow . . .' gasped Dickon. 'Coward . . . cheat!'

'So! Coward is it?'

Tom lifted his foot to kick the helpless Dickon.

'Tom!' Will pushed between then. 'Stop it now, please, before someone gets hurt.'

'What . . . do you . . . mean . . .? I . . . *am* . . . hurt!'

Dickon was on his knees, still trying to control his laboured breathing. He glared up at Tom through his tears. 'As soon as I'm . . . recovered . . . I'll give you such a beating . . .'

Tom slapped his hands on his thighs, and roared with exaggerated laughter. 'And who will fight for you, *squire?*' he sneered. 'For you don't seem able to fight for yourself, do you?'

'I'll have you thrashed!' said Dickon, getting unsteadily to his feet. 'I'll have you thrashed to within an inch of your life!'

'Stop it, I beg you!' said Will. 'Make up, be friends – *please*. We came out for an afternoon's sport, not to fight each other!'

'He started it!' shouted Tom.

'Liar!' snapped Dickon.

'Impostor!' yelled Tom.

'Insolent upstart!' bellowed Dickon, his anger overcoming the pain.

Will looked from one to the other; from the sneering apprentice to the scowling cousin.

'Stop it,' he pleaded.

'Never!'

'Make peace . . .?'

'*Never!*'

'I demand an apology!' shouted Dickon.

'I refuse!' bellowed Tom.

'There is only one course a gentleman can take,' shouted Dickon. 'A duel!'

'*No!*' wailed Will.

'Yes!' said Tom. 'I agree – a duel!'

'And you will be my second, Will!' said Dickon.

'No, he shall be mine!' shouted Tom.

'He's my cousin!' said Dickon haughtily.

'He's my friend!' said Tom, pointedly.

'*Stop it!*' Will had tears in his eyes. They were fools, nothing but fools!

'Will, you shall choose,' said Dickon. 'How shall we fight?'

'Yes, Will,' Tom agreed. 'You shall decide – what will it be?'

Will stood in the middle of the two, appalled. A fight – a *real* fight with cudgels, or staffs, or – heaven forbid – knives! And all for nothing; all because of a day's sport! What could he do?

He turned away, trying to control his fear, trying to think of a way out. *Fools!* he thought again.

'Well . . .?' demanded Dickon.

'What's it to be?' demanded Tom.

More time, thought Will. He could feel an idea beginning to stir, beginning to take shape just beyond his grasp. There *was* an answer, a way out.

'You will abide by what I say?'

'I will!' declared Tom.

'I swear!' said Dickon pompously.

Will paused. The idea was rushing towards him, closer and clearer: fools capering with balls on sticks . . . the time his father had taken him to Asherton one Shrove Tuesday, and they'd seen . . . The idea was suddenly visible now, fully formed – not a duel but *sport!*

Will took a deep breath. 'Your weapon will be . . .' he paused again.

'Well . . .?' demanded Tom.

'Well . . .?' demanded Dickon.

'A pig's bladder!'

'*What?*' both boys gaped.

91

'A game of football,' explained Will. 'That will be your battle.'

'No!'

'Never!'

'Yes!' said Will, firmly. 'You both promised to abide by my decision. This is it: you have one week to raise two teams – those will be your armies. And your fight will be . . . a game of football!'

He stopped again. His brain was racing, charging ahead of him like a bolting horse or a sprinting dog. He fought to control it, to slow it back down to a normal walking pace. He took a deep breath and continued: 'And if you cannot raise the teams – then that is an end to the matter: you will shake hands and be friends once again!'

The following Saturday morning, Will woke early. It was a little before dawn, just in time to hear his mother's cockerel crow for the first time. His brother Gilbert slept on, undisturbed beside him. But Will could not settle on the hard, straw-filled mattress.

He climbed out of bed, the tails of his grimy shirt flapping at the backs of his knees, and crept across the bare wooden boards to the window. He looked out across the street. The eastern sky was beginning to glow pink. It would soon be time. He crept back to the bed and pulled on his doublet and hose. Then he sat on the bed, listening for Tom's step in the narrow passageway.

All week the opposing armies had grown. Dickon had recruited the heartiest lads from the grammar school; Tom had marshalled the toughest apprentices – not only glovers, which was Tom's trade, but boys from other trades. There were two or three tanners, who stank of the curing ponds – no one would want to get into a close ruck with them. And there were a couple of young butchers, who were built almost as solidly as the great sides of beef they could haul around and chop up as easily as if they were bundles of kindling.

The field of battle had also been agreed. The game was to be played between the Clopton Bridge and Holy Trinity Church, along Waterside, the road which ran beside the river and marked the northern edge of the town. It was ideal. Waterside was so close to the Avon that there were few houses, so little chance of an outraged shopkeeper or an interfering nosy parker calling out the Watch.

The rules of the game were simple, like those of the Asherton match Will had once seen. Each team had a goal to aim for: the apprentices had to try to carry the pig's bladder ball to the bridge, and the schoolboys had to ground it at the churchyard gate. There was no limit on the number of players on each side, and the ball could be kicked, punched, thrown or carried; so could the players.

There was the muffled creak of a floorboard outside the bedroom. Will tensed. There was a soft scratch at the door. Barely breathing, Will inched open the door. The dim, lanky figure on the landing beckoned to him, and began tiptoeing down the narrow wooden stairs. Will followed. Every step was heart-stopping. If his father discovered them creeping out, there would certainly be a sound beating for both boys. Will sighed. They would face a beating anyway, whether they woke Will's father or not. There was work to be done, and Will's father stood no slackness from either his apprentice or his son – especially since the money troubles had begun.

Tom and Will slipped out of the back door and ran past the stinking pools in which the skins, which Will's father and Tom made into gloves, soaked until they were as soft as the finest velvet.

They walked quickly along Henley Street.

'Well?' hissed Tom. 'Are you with me or against me, Will? It's one or the other.'

It was the question Will had been dreading. All week they had been asking him – first Tom, then Dickon:

'*My team or his . . .*'

'Me or him . . .'

'*Friend or foe . . .*'

'Which is it to be?'

'*Which is it to be?*'

It was the day of the game, and Will *still* didn't know.

'Well . . .?' repeated Tom.

'Hurry or we'll be late,' said Will, ignoring the question.

He jogged round the corner in the High Street, with Tom close behind. They sped past the darkened shops and silent houses into Chapel Street. With every second, the weak morning light was getting stronger, and the moment when Will would be forced to take sides was getting ever closer. Which team *would* he be on?

'I want neither,' he muttered to himself. 'Don't they understand?'

Will and Tom turned right up Chapel Lane. Up ahead, at the agreed spot, midway between the church and the bridge, two gangs of about twenty boys stood facing each other, glowering.

At the head of one gang stood Dickon, a blown-up pig's bladder in his hand.

'Come on, you grammar school milksop! Or are you too much of a molly-coddle to see this through?' shouted one of the apprentices.

Dickon bunched his fists together. Tom took his place at the front of his team.

'We're ready!' called Tom. 'Ready to crack your skulls until you plead *Mercy! Mercy! Mercy!* Like the mewling little maids you are!'

'Begin!' shouted one of Tom's team. 'Begin!' echoed another. 'Begin! Begin! Begin!'

Tom turned to Will. 'It was Will's suggestion,' he bellowed over the apprentices' chanting. 'Let him start us off!'

There were cries of 'Yes!' from the apprentices. From the schoolboys' side a voice shouted, 'Who cares for the ball – let's just give them the thrashing they deserve!' followed by a cheer from a handful of the other boys.

With a curt nod, Dickon flung the pig's bladder to Will. Will fumbled the catch and dropped the bladder. Blushing, Will picked up the bladder. It was round and greyish-yellow: it felt slightly spongy beneath his fingers, as if it could do with a couple more hearty puffs. But it was too late to worry about that now.

Squinting with concentration, Will threw the ball as hard as he could at a spot in the dirt road between Dickon and Tom. With a great roar both gangs of boys rushed at each other. They locked together in a single struggling, grunting mass of flailing fists and bellowing voices.

'Where's the ball?' shouted a voice that sounded to Will like Tom's.

'At the bottom!' shouted back a heavily built red-haired boy, who was digging like a huge mole at the mass of struggling bodies. He lifted the ball high with a shout, cut short by the fist of an opponent crunching into his jaw. He disappeared down into the struggling mayhem still clutching the ball.

Will had been trying to avoid the struggling kicking mass and work his way round the scrum to the far side, by the river, where he thought he'd be safe. He'd just reached the far side of the road when the ball squirted out of the bottom of the scrum and rolled to a stop at his feet. For an endless fraction of a second Will gazed at the ball in horror before being engulfed in the howling mob. As the wall of bodies swallowed him, a fist hit Will in the throat and made him gag, his legs were knocked from under him and he was rolling helplessly backwards. He felt a kick in his back and then the awful stifling weight of someone falling across his back.

'Get off me!' he screamed. 'You're crushing me!'

The mass of bodies swayed, then pushed back the way it had come. Will frantically burrowed his way on all fours to the outside of the pack. He didn't care who he was gouging and clawing and scratching on his way out, nor did he care where he was clawing and gouging them. Tears of pure fear were running down his cheeks. He knew his life was in danger in that awful, heaving, suffocating mass of bodies. He knew that the enormous beast – the many-headed, many-limbed howling monster that the schoolboys and apprentices had become – could crush and tear and kill without a second thought.

Will fought his way out onto the green mossy bank beside the river. He hauled himself to his feet, sobbing and gasping for air just as the mob swayed back in his direction.

'No!' screamed Will. '*No!*'

An elbow smashed into his chest. Someone's knee knocked him behind the legs. As Will turned round to protect his front, someone else gave him a shove in the back. Will felt his feet start to slide down the bank. He whirled his arms desperately in the air to try and keep his balance. He teetered on the brink, frantically trying to clutch onto a handhold in the empty air. Then with a final, despairing, yodelling cry, Will fell into the filthy river with an enormous splash.

The coldness of the water drove the breath out of Will's lungs. He struggled to get his footing on the slimy, shelving river bottom.

'Help!' he shouted. 'I've—'

His feet slipped and his knees buckled again. He splashed face down in the water, taking in another foul-tasting mouthful of brown water.

'Splouff! Arcch!'

He spat out the water and began thrashing his way along the bank towards a small clump of willow trees where the muddy slope was less steep.

'*I command you to stop!*'

Will heard a familiar voice boom above the shouting and cursing of the football players.

'Stop!' it bellowed again. 'As Alderman of this town, I command you: *Stop at once!*'

All through Will's childhood, the stern voice of his father had stopped even the most harmless of childish pranks as swiftly as the stinging cut of the birch rods which his father kept hanging on the kitchen wall. That same voice now stopped the game of football.

There was a sudden, shocked silence. Will cowered beneath the overhanging willow branches.

'Captain of the Watch – *arrest them!*'

There was a sound of shuffling feet, and a few muffled snuffles and whimpers. Will pressed himself against the cold, slimy banks of the river.

'And where is my son?' demanded the voice. 'Where is the one who has brought disgrace upon my household!' he bellowed.

Will closed his eyes and held his breath.

'*Well?*'

There was no reply.

'Let him hear this,' boomed the voice. 'He has brought shame upon his family, and let him be sure that he will be sorely punished when he returns. And the longer he hides, the harsher will be his punishment!'

There was another long pause.

'Take them back!' he snapped to the constables of the Watch. Will listened to the shuffle of feet, gradually fading as the schoolboys and apprentices were marched away from the river side. He stood, shivering in the icy water, for one minute . . . two . . . three . . . four . . . five.

Then there was a crack of a twig and the sound of someone slithering down the bank.

Will shut his eyes and tried to press himself into the bank.

'What have we here?'

It was light, musical voice. Will turned round. Peering down at him was a short, plump young man dressed in a bright scarlet doublet, with a bundle of linen under his arm.

'Is it an eel? Or maybe a particularly slimy newt? Eh?'

The young man laughed and held out a hand. He helped Will out of the water and onto the bank.

'So, you were in the riot and got clean away, eh?' asked the man.

'It wasn't a riot,' said Will, horrified. 'It was a football match.'

'Is that so?' asked the fat man, with mock solemnity. 'And, pray, whose idea was it to play this football match?'

Will sighed. 'Mine,' he admitted in a soft voice.

'Speak up!' said the man. 'No use speaking if you can't be heard. I'll ask you again: whose idea was it?'

'Mine,' admitted Will again, in a louder voice.

'Better,' said the man thoughtfully. 'A good voice – a little reedy, perhaps. No good for singing, but adequate for an attendant lord, or perhaps a messenger of no great consequence.'

Will stared at the young man in the garish clothes. What was he talking about?

'So you were the playmaster of this little shenanigans,' said the man. 'I was just come down to wash our costumes here in the stream, when I see a full-scale riot going on and the Watch pelting along the lane to crack a few heads. So I say to myself: time to hide, Will Kemp, until matters are settled. So I hid behind this clump of trees, and merry amusement it was to be sure, especially your dive into the River Avon!' And he laughed heartily.

'Costumes?' asked Will.

'Yes, lad,' replied Will Kemp, patting the pile. 'Tonight we play the comedy of *Damon and Pithias* at the Swan Inn.' He pointed to one of the two squat thatched buildings standing beside the bridge. 'And if I don't get these washed and dried before this afternoon I'll be capering with a toe up my backside!'

'Players?' asked Will. 'Are you travelling players?'

'Aye, lad,' said Kemp. 'Or, as some call us, stout beggars and vagabonds. This evening we play here at Stratford, then we're away before midnight, and tomorrow we play at . . .'

'You leave tonight?' Will interrupted.

'We surely do.'

One of Will's lightning ideas came to him.

'Take me with you,' he begged. 'I must leave the town tonight, or . . . or . . . or . . .'

'Or you'll get the beating you so richly deserve?' suggested Will Kemp and guffawed again. 'So you'd rather go for a player than face the music – is that it?'

Will nodded.

Kemp laughed again. Then he shook his head. 'It would do you no good and it would do no good for us, either. I'm sorry, lad, if we were to take a rich man's son – a grammar school boy too, I would guess – the Watch would be on us before we left the parish boundaries. We'd all be getting a thrashing – you, me and all the rest of my company. No, lad. It's not worth it. Besides, the life of a player's not the life for the likes of you, I can promise you that.'

'But *please* . . .' implored Will.

Kemp shook his head again. 'No, my fine young gentleman. You stay here and take the beating that's coming to you. And when you're grown, then you may come to the Swan Inn one fine evening and watch old Will Kemp caper his way through some fine entertainment for your pleasure. And you can clap, and cheer, and spare a silver penny to give to old Will

Kemp, and in the morning think no more about it than a pleasant dream that gave pleasure and hurt no one – unlike your game of football!'

Kemp squatted down by the river and began to soak the soiled costumes.

Will got to his feet, shivering, river water running off his clothes. He clambered up the bank. Then he turned and looked down at the tubby figure, sluicing the clothes in the grimy water. Then he looked over the meadows towards the Swan Inn, and the bridge, and the road that led out of Stratford.

'One day . . .' he muttered to himself. 'One day I will run and run and run and never come back.'

He looked down at the scarlet back bent over its laundry. 'One day, Will Kemp, we will meet again,' he declared in his grandest voice, 'and then you'll be sorry you didn't take me with you today!'

Will turned and began limping towards the road.

Kemp gave a roar of laughter and clapped his wet hands together.

'Bravo!' he called out to Will's retreating back. 'A splendid exit line, young sir! *Bravo!* Maybe you *do* have the makings of a player after all. But one thing I can promise you – you'll never make a *football* player!'

And Will Kemp roared with laughter once again.

Strikers and Keepers

John Goodwin

The huge crowd were up on their feet. 'Penalty! Penalty!' they shouted. The referee blew his whistle and pointed to the spot. The crowd cheered and held their arms aloft. Now surely the winning goal would be scored and for their team it would be triumph yet again. Still their cheering echoed round the stadium and mingled with chants of 'Paggio . . . Paggio . . .'

Carlo Paggio, the team's captain, stepped forward and placed the ball on the spot. The crowd were quiet now. All the players stood quite still. Paggio too stood still. He looked at the ball, then at the goal, and then back at the ball again. He shook his hands by his sides and then took three very deliberate steps back. All eyes were on the ball.

He ran forward swiftly and hit the ball hard and true as only a great player can. It was right on target and zoomed towards the bottom right corner of the net. Perfection. Yet a blurred shape in green was hurling itself towards the ball. The goalkeeper! Arms were flung forward and in a rolling mass of ball and gloves and goalkeeper's body the penalty was . . .

I switched off the video and dressed for school. Tuesday is can't wait day. It's straight downstairs. Sneak past Mum and Amber's bedrooms and don't make a sound on the creaking floorboard to wake the dog. Pull the magazine out of the letter box and stuff your fingers in the letter box flap to stop it shutting with a crash. Then fly upstairs as fast and quietly as you can, clutching the magazine tight in your fist. Close your bedroom door without a sound and then breathe more easily. Get ready for your fist full of football fantasy and magic. For Tuesday is the day of *Score* and its free football stickers.

Only it wasn't. Not this Tuesday. The letter box was closed, its mouth shut tight. No football magazine stuck out of its jaws. No stickers to add to the collection.

I stared hard at the letter box, half expecting the flap to open at any second and the roll of the magazine to be pushed through. I waited for ages. I waited until my toes were blue with cold and my teeth started to chatter.

No magazine.

I levered open the flap of the letter box to look through it and see if the magazine was lying outside on the pavement. It wasn't. My fingers slipped on the letter box flap and it shut with a crash. There was only one thing for it.

I opened the door as quietly as I could and set off along the pavement faster than the players come out of the tunnel at the start of a match. I had one target in my view: Goodall's Paper Shop. There was just enough time before school, but I'd have to run all the way.

The trees in Lime Grove were the players of the other team. I passed three and they didn't move a centimetre. I was just too quick for their lumbering branches to catch me. The goal was in sight. I went round a fourth – I was flying.

Then the defence showed their dirty play. A huge root of a tree burst viciously through a crack in the pavement. It was a brute of a root, deep from the black earth. Then it was round my ankle and pulling me crashing to the ground.

'Penalty! Penalty!' screamed the crowd. First I was Carlo Paggio, the striker, and then I was in the goal-keeper's green strip, hurling myself sideways along the High Street and straight into Goodall's Paper Shop. My gloved goalkeeper hands were ready to grab that fistful of football stickers. Behind the counter stood Mrs Goodall in her referee's black uniform.

'Steady on, lad,' she said, taking a pencil from behind her ear and licking the end of it.

'I want . . .'

'I know what you want,' she said, licking the pencil for a second time. 'You came in here last week, didn't you?' she asked as her thick black pencil scrawled the numbers of houses onto a huge bundle of newspapers.

'Yes,' I said.

'Then you'll know the paper boy delivers your papers.'

'Yes,' I repeated.

'So why have you come here?' she asked, lifting an even bigger bundle of newspapers onto the shop counter. 'Actually, I know why,' she said, without looking at me. 'It's those football stickers, isn't it?'

I nodded a silent nod.

'And your stickers are in the magazine which the paper boy has with him.'

'Oh,' I said and took a step back towards the shop door.

'Here, I've got a spare packet of them,' said Mrs Goodall as she pulled a set of stickers out of her pocket and threw them towards me. I dived forward and caught them with the best goalkeeper grip I could manage.

'For me?' I asked her.

'Well, they're not for Gary Lineker, are they? Now take them out of my way. I need to get on with these papers.'

I was out of the shop in a stride. Once outside I ripped open the packet of stickers with my teeth. Ben Buck. I'd got him. Vinny Capstick. Everybody's got him ten times over. Two to go. Please, *please*! I'll do anything if it could be him. Not be rude to Amber for a whole week. I'll promise anything, if only . . . Giorgio Fabrizi. Oh no. He's the worst player ever. And now for the last one. The big one. I can't look. It won't be him. I know it won't.

I don't believe it!

Look again. Pinch yourself. It is.

Mika Tailer

The sticker everybody wants and nobody, but nobody, has got so far. Except me. And I'm going to keep him. You bet I am. Mika, the only goalkeeper to save three penalties in a World Cup final. Mika, my hero.

I just stood and stared at his face. I had been trying to collect his sticker ever since the magazine had first come out. I put my finger on the sticker and let it go right round the shape of his face. My finger was coming up to the top of his head for a second time when the expression on Mika's face seemed to change. It was smiling. You might think I was dreaming, but I tell you it's true.

Then my eyes started to go blurry and I couldn't see straight. I put the sticker carefully into my trouser pocket and ran all the way to school without stopping.

I knew that sticker would bring me luck. It had to. Now the kid they all called 'wimp head' would show them a thing or two. They were in for a few surprises.

When it was time for our football lesson, I hid the sticker in my sock, ran out of the changing room and sprinted up and down the pitch. Knocker and his mates started to giggle and call out, 'Wimp head . . . wimp head . . .'

But I didn't listen, because it was time for the wimp to triumph. No more miskicking for me. No more feeble attempts at heading the ball. This time I was a striker – a striker with a red hot sticker in his sock.

Mr Brailsford, our PE teacher, gathered us round and picked two teams like he always did in the football lesson.

'Charlton, Wayne, Woody, Dannie, Josh, Edward and Ben . . .' Mr Brailsford's picking was just about complete. 'Oh, and James, Ryan and . . . Jack.'

There were only two players left without a team. One was Knocker, a giant of a boy with size ten boots. The other was me – a skinny little lad they called wimp head.

'Would you believe it, I almost forgot you two,' he said with a grin. I'd thought perhaps we were going to get the red card before we'd even started.

'There's an odd number today. You can play in the same team. We can swap someone over at half-time.'

Knocker glared at me and said, 'Oh sir, can't he play in the other team?'

'No,' said Mr Brailsford firmly.

'But he's useless. A wet wimpy spider with . . .'

But Mr Brailsford didn't let Knocker finish his sentence and blew his whistle for the start of the match.

We kicked off. I positioned myself as striker and ran up towards the other team's penalty area. I ran fast and hard and found myself with a bit of open space around me. I eyed up their goalie, Josh. He wasn't that good. He only went in goal because nobody else in their team wanted to. Surely I could put a shot past him and find the back of the net. All I needed was one good chance. One neat pass from midfield, a quick dart up the pitch, and the shot was on. We could be one–nil up, no sweat.

I waited for ages in that open space by myself. Nothing happened. No neat pass came from midfield. No pass came at all. I might as well have been on a different planet for all the part I played in the match. Most of the play happened in the other half of the field, and we were soon two–nil down.

When we did get the ball, Knocker had it. It was as if it was glued to the end of his size tens and there was nobody else in the team but him. He was the biggest kid in the class. Big boots and big mouth. He ran all over the pitch. He barged and pushed, then ran some more, lost control of the ball or shot miles wide of the goal.

Out of nowhere we got a free kick. Mr Brailsford blew his whistle hard.

'Free kick,' he said to me. 'You take it, Sam. Give it a big kick upfield.'

He placed the ball on the ground.

'Not him!' shouted Knocker. 'He couldn't kick his way out of a bag of chips!'

Some of the kids began to giggle, and I could hear Josh far away in the goal with his loud, stupid laugh. The more he laughed, the worse it was.

'Don't take any notice of the rest, Sam,' said Mr Brailsford. 'Just give it one big kick.'

I looked at the ball and tried not to think about being a wimp. I tried really hard, but somehow I just couldn't block them out. My foot hit the ground in front of the ball and instead of it flying high into the air, it just trickled forward a few centimetres and then stopped. I could hear loud booing coming from Josh in goal.

Mr Brailsford blew his whistle.

'Half-time. Change ends... and cut out that booing.'

The second half started. Mr Brailsford put Knocker into the other team. I ran upfield just like before, and just like before nobody passed the ball to me. The other team scored and we were three–nil down. It was a complete waste of time. I was so busy feeling sorry for myself that I hadn't noticed the ball roll towards me. A perfect pass from midfield. I just stood and stared at the ball. Behind me, the others were shouting and yelling. Their cries were getting closer.

'*Kickit, kickitup. Goforgoal. Samkickitup.*'

If I didn't do something soon it would be too late.

I ran forward three steps and looked at the goal. It seemed miles away. Surely I couldn't shoot for goal from this far back! Behind me, the rest of the players were so close. The ground was shaking as two size-ten boots pounded the turf a few metres away.

It was now or never. The sticker in my sock was

burning hot. Then my whole leg was burning, and pulling itself slowly back.

I could see the studs of Knocker's size tens out of the corner of my eye. My leg went forward at galactic speed. It struck the ball at seventy miles an hour. Off zoomed the ball goalwards – right on target.

Josh saw it coming. He wasn't booing now. That volley had shut him up for sure. He placed himself in the centre of the goal and watched the ball like a hawk. His hands and body were ready to block its movement when the right moment came. Yet the ball was swerving and gathering speed as it travelled through the air.

Faster and faster it went. I wanted to shout out and tell everybody that it was impossible to stop a shot like this one. That Josh had better move out of the way before he was killed. But before I could say a word, the ball was near the goal and heading for the top corner of the net.

Yet it missed the net and crashed into the goalpost. Crunch went the post and down fell the net as the goalpost was broken into two pieces.

All the players stood on the pitch and looked at the broken mess. Mr Brailsford was leading Josh away from the tangled web of net and post, and Josh was scratching his head in a daze. I just stared at it all silently. Had *I* done this? I should have been dancing round the pitch with my shirt pulled over my head like they do on the telly. Instead I just felt numb. It was like a hurricane had struck.

'What a strike!' said Mr Brailsford, excitedly. 'The strike of the century. I've never seen a kick like it. We shall all have to wear crash helmets next. How on earth did you kick the ball like that, Sam?'

For some questions it's best not to try and find an answer.

The flu came. Loads of kids were off school with it. Josh even fainted in assembly and had to be taken home in one of the teacher's cars. It meant the school football team were short of players. Things were so desperate I was picked for the eleven for the match on Wednesday afternoon.

Mr Brailsford gave us a pep talk in the changing room before the match.

'This is the big one,' he said. 'You know the Under-12s haven't won a match all season. Some of the other school teams have had victory after victory, but all we've done is crash from defeat to defeat. We're going to win today, aren't we?'

All our voices spoke as one. 'Yes, sir!'

It was a tight match. Nil–nil and well into the second half. But the opposition were spending more and more time in our goal mouth. We managed to clear attack after attack, but it could only be a matter of time before they would find the back of our net. Somebody had to do something. Somebody with a sticker in his sock. Mr Brailsford's words at half-time were pounding in my head.

'Wear your shirts with pride.'

It was up to me. It was time for me to show some pride. To stop playing like a scared wimp. The next time the ball came anywhere near me, I'd do it. Mika wouldn't let me down. I could crack the ball all the length of the pitch just like last time and smack it right into their goal. If I kicked from near our goal it would be safe enough not to break the goalposts. Then we'd be one–nil up with the game in the bag.

They won another corner. This was it. The moment I'd waited for all match. I positioned myself on the goal line, waiting for the sticker to burn hot in my sock and for my leg to get strong and powerful. Only it didn't seem to be working. The ball was almost on me when I began to jump. Up in the air I went, propelled by Mika power. Higher and higher I climbed. I had a sudden panic. Maybe I was going into orbit. Look out, Jupiter, here I come!

Out shot my arms like a spring uncoiled as I caught the ball just before it hit the back of the net.

'Penalty! Penalty!' screamed the opposition.

I fell to the ground clutching the ball.

'You caught the ball . . . but you're not the goalie,' said a quiet voice. 'You've given away a penalty, and now we'll lose the game.'

I heard what they were saying, but my legs were out of control. The sticker power had taken over. I was up on my feet, clutching the ball to my chest. The ref's whistle was blowing, but I took no notice.

'Penalty, Sam!' shouted Mr Brailsford. 'Put the ball down.' But I didn't. I ran two steps with it.

Now everybody was shouting, 'Put the ball down!'

Still I ignored them. I pulled my arm back and hurled the ball high in the air. Miles high. And now I was shouting. The words just said themselves.

'Go on . . . Go for it . . . Chase that ball. Let's have a goal. Go for it, Knocker . . . Go for goal.'

Only Knocker didn't chase out. Instead he ran to me and shouted, 'You stupid wimp. You've lost us the game!'

Then he pulled back his fist and punched me in the mouth.

I ripped the sticker into tiny pieces and watched them fall all over my bedroom floor. This was the end of football for me. I'd let everybody down so badly. Mr Brailsford, the team, everybody. I'd made such a fool of myself. To think I could score a winning goal like that. It was pathetic. Mr Brailsford's record of defeats was getting worse. I'd made a promise that he could rely on me, and this was how I paid him back.

I looked at the bits of sticker strewn over the floor. Mika wasn't to blame. He was a world-class goalie. What would he do if the ball zoomed towards him, heading for the net? Of course he'd jump up and catch it with both hands. That was his job. It was why he was famous.

My mother's voice called out from downstairs.

'Sam . . . Sam.'

I didn't answer.

'Sam . . . somebody to see you.'

'I'm not in!' I shouted back.

A few minutes later there was a knock on my bedroom door. 'Go away,' I said.

It went quiet and then a small voice said, 'It's me, Sam . . . Charlton. I've come with some good news.'

'Go away, Charlton.'

'Knocker has been banned from the team and you've been picked for the next match . . . only this time you're the goalie.'

I ran along the pavement. I ran past the trees in Lime Grove and their lumbering branches, their outstretched arms ready to trip me up. But I needed to run faster or Goodall's Paper Shop would be closed for the day and then it would be too late. I needed another Mika sticker. If I was going to play again in the school team I had to have zap power. I couldn't do without it.

Into the High Street I sprinted, just as Mrs Goodall was turning the notice in the window from *Open* to *Closed*.

'You've cut it fine,' she said, moving off towards the shop counter.

'I ran all the way,' I said, trying to get my breath back.

'I can see that,' she said. 'You're all of a lather.'

I didn't know what a lather was, but I knew what I had to ask for.

'I was wondering if . . .'

'No,' she said, turning off the light above a display cabinet. 'Sold out.'

She took off her referee's black uniform and hung it on a nail in the wall.

'I need some stickers . . .'

'I said we've sold out. Last lot went ages ago.' Then she peered closer at me. 'What do you want them for anyway?'

'I want the luck,' I said.

'There's no luck in them,' she said gently. 'The only real luck you need is in that head of yours.'

'Oh,' I said, not making any sense of what she was saying. Her hand moved towards the light switches. The shop went dark and I found myself outside, feeling numb.

It seemed a long way back home. Mrs Goodall's words were pounding over and over in my head. How could I manage without the sticker in my sock?

How could I make my own luck? How could I become a great goalie for the school team?

By now a bit of a wind was blowing down Lime Grove. It made a strange noise in the branches of the trees. Not a scary sort of noise, but a noise like people talking. And the talking was growing louder and now the sound filled the air. People were clapping and chanting and waving. They were up on their feet.

'Penalty! Penalty!' they screamed.

The imaginary ref looked very much like Mrs Goodall in her black uniform. She blew her whistle and pointed to the spot. It went very quiet now. I pushed my fingers to the very tips of my goalie gloves and took a deep breath. Somehow I had to save the penalty. If I did that, we would win our first game.

'To the right . . . he's going to kick it low to the right,' said a voice inside my head. I took another very deep breath, stood quite still and waited for my moment. Then the whistle went and the ball was struck cleanly, bang on target. It seemed a certain goal. I dived for the ball, just like Mika would. My arms were flung forward, and in a rolling mass of ball and gloves and goalkeeper's body . . .

The penalty was saved!

Lyon Heart

Ann Ruffell

There had been a student demonstration on the streets, a police chase round the city, a multiple crash on the Boulevard (Lyon's ring road) and a bin-men's strike. And that was just for starters.

But here, in the flat on the outskirts of Lyon, one of France's biggest cities, I was so bored that I wanted to push somebody into one of the overflowing dustbins just to see what they'd do about it.

It had seemed such a good idea at first. Dad had to go to a conference, and our friends who lived in Lyon invited the whole family to come too. Mum wanted to go, and they couldn't just abandon me, so I got a whole week off school when everyone else was still glumly slogging through projects that they'd long ago lost interest in.

'*South of France?*' they said. 'You lucky thing, Jane.'

'Well, it's only sort of middle-to-south,' I told them.

'Can you get me in your suitcase?'

'Send us a postcard!'

But all the time we'd been here, Mum and Dad had spent their time talking to their friends in bad French which I couldn't understand, eating strange food (including terrifyingly stinky cheese), drinking wine that made Mum go all giggly, and going out in the golden light of Lyon to look at museums and boring churches.

Michel, who was the only son, was at school all day. Like I should have been if I'd had any sense and said I'd stay with Laura for the week. It makes you glad to be English when you see them going off to school at crack of dawn. They start at *eight o'clock* and don't finish till half past five! And then they've got loads of homework to do.

I wrote that on my postcard to Laura to cheer her up.

Michel was all right, I suppose, but like I said, I didn't see a lot of him.

Until Saturday.

They were talking about the bomb on the Paris Métro. And talking half French and half English, because Dad was feeling a bit fierce about it and couldn't find the words in French.

'It's terrible that you have to throw a bomb and risk killing people to make yourself heard,' he said.

Michel's father made French noises like a kind of puffing spit. 'A bomb is meant to kill, and to kill – that is never reasonable.'

'Nobody was hurt, which was lucky, but if nobody listens to reason about important issues...' my mother began.

And Michel's mother stood up for her. The argument went on well into the afternoon, and you could see they were all enjoying themselves immensely. And practising their French and English like mad.

We were to go home next day. *Thank goodness,* I thought to myself. I've never had such a yawning holiday in my life. But instead of making my last evening something wonderful to be remembered, my parents announced they were going out to dinner. Without me.

Out. To dinner.

As if they hadn't spent all the rest of their time *eating!*

Michel, they said, would look after me.

Big deal.

Michel wanted to go to a football match. 'It's a match between Lyon and our deadly rivals, St Etienne,' he explained to Dad. 'Every Lyon supporter will be there!'

Football! I ask you! I could just hear my friends when we got back: 'So – what did you do in France?' They would be expecting me to say we did things like hunting in the forests for wild boar, like Asterix and Obelix. Or picking grapes in the fields. Or going clubbing. Not going to a boring football match! It was about the last thing I would have chosen to do on my last day.

I said no.

'Come on, Janey, you'll enjoy it,' said my father.

I said no.

'But Jane,' said my mother, 'it's only polite . . .'

'It would be more polite of him to take me somewhere *I'd* like to go,' I sulked. 'Why can't I stay here by myself if he wants to go?'

'You're too young! You certainly can't stay here by yourself. And anyway, where *would* you like to go?'

But that was the trouble. I didn't know where, and I'd used up all the French I knew a hundred times over and was definitely running out of conversation. I suppose I was lucky that Michel knew a bit more English than I knew French, though he had a nasty habit of laughing at me when I did try.

So I just shrugged my shoulders in what I hoped was a proper French way. 'I suppose I'll have to go,' I said.

Mum sighed, and Dad looked angry, but I'd *said* I would, hadn't I, so what were they moaning about?

'Enjoy yourselves!' said Mum brightly as I followed Michel to the door, carrying my small back-pack with a spare sweater, sandwiches and a plastic bottle of mineral water in it. Sandwiches because we weren't getting any dinner, and water because Michel said they wouldn't let us in with drinks cans because of the bomb in Paris last week.

It was just the same as home on match days. As the bus got nearer to the stadium more and more people got on, and more and more people could be seen, all walking in the same direction, towards a blaze of floodlights.

'Don't people queue?' I asked Michel as he joined a crowd round the first of a row of ticket booths.

'Queue? In France?' He laughed, and pushed evilly at the group in front of us. I grabbed onto his coat. There were far too many people here. The road was packed with people, walking, pushing, laughing.

Just as Michel got to the booth, the woman behind the counter slapped a large book in front of the window to show she was closed, and the crowd surged to the next one.

'Well, she might have said!' I muttered indignantly, but Michel simply laughed and began to elbow his way to the front again.

You won't believe this, but *each* time we got near a booth they decided to run out of tickets and we had to move on to the next one. I began to feel quite cheerful. Perhaps we'd never get a ticket, then we'd have to go home, and I could go to my room and read a book or something.

But from the fifth one Michel emerged, triumphantly waving a pair of tickets.

And we joined another crush.

This was definitely the worst night of my life. If this was what football was about – standing in huge crowds of people, absolutely all of whom were taller than me so that the only view of anything I could get was the small of someone's back – then I'd rather not, thank you.

'*La police*,' Michel bawled into my ear.

'What?'

'Searching. I think because of the bomber. They do not find him yet.'

'He's in Paris anyway, isn't he?' I couldn't see why they were searching us here, in Lyon, when the bloke was five hundred kilometres away in the capital of France.

But they were certainly searching for something. As the shove of people swayed, centimetre by centimetre, nearer the stadium gates, I saw them on top of the stand. With guns. You could see them quite clearly, silhouetted against the orange and pink evening light.

Mum and Dad would definitely *not* have wanted me to go if they'd known. But there was no way I could get home now – it was clear Michel wasn't bothered. Perhaps it happens all the time at French football matches.

We reached the gate. The ticket collectors ripped tickets. We joined another crush. Security men searched our bags and took away our bottles of water. Michel protested, but it happened to everyone: there were heaps of leaking bottles of Vittel muddying the

121

ground. 'In case we make a bomb with one,' explained Michel, and we laughed at the thought of water bombs crashing down on the teams.

Another crush. And policemen and women doing body searches.

'I hope we get in for the kick-off,' Michel was saying anxiously as we milled up the steps to the back of the stand.

Who cared about kick-offs? I thought. *There* was something to tell my friends! Guns *and* body-searches! Better than a pop concert!

As we fought our way to a sort of plastic cushion on a concrete step, men were striding up the steps with sheets of blue paper, thrusting them into our hands.

'What's that for?' I asked Michel suspiciously. I had a horrible memory of school trips. You go out for a fun day, and they spoil it by giving you sheets of paper to write about it.

'To wave,' explained Michel.

So we waved, and great flowers of colour – blue from our stand, red from the next – flashed over the crowd.

And at last the match began.

I settled down for a couple of hours of boredom, and wondered what the toilets would be like. (I found out. I won't describe them. You'll be sick.)

Half my mind watched the pattern of red-and-blue and green figures on the emerald pitch, while I thought about our early start tomorrow to catch the plane back home. It would be cold in England. Grey skies, grey buildings, grey school uniform.

For goodness' *sake* – is that all you do at a football

match? Run up and down after that stupid ball, trying to kick it into a net?

Michel began to explain that there was more to it than that. He pointed to a red-and-blue-clad player, who even I could see had deliberately kicked the ball off the pitch, and told me that this was the right strategy for this moment. I couldn't see it myself, but the whole of the red-and-blues surged up to our end, and suddenly one in black, who had been sort of loafing about by the goalposts, sprang into action but didn't quite make it.

The crowd went mad.

Michel leapt to his feet, clapping and shouting.

There were two people sitting by me, the only people apart from me in the whole of the stadium who didn't jump up and down. We looked at each other sympathetically. *These mad football fiends!* we said with our shrugs. I wondered who'd dragged them along.

But somehow, now that our team had got a goal, I began to be interested. The patterns of players started to make some kind of sense.

'Why did he do that?' I said indignantly as a green-clad Stéphanois (what they called the St Etienners) shoved one of our side to the ground to get to the ball.

Michel stopped his insulting chant to answer me. 'They try to win by cheating, because they are not as good as us,' he said contemptuously.

But as I watched, there was a sort of motorway pile-up somewhere in the middle of the pitch, where a heap of players fell on top of one another and a medical team rushed out with a stretcher and took one of our red-and-blue ones off.

And suddenly, across the pitch, there was a great movement of people from the corner to the centre.

'What's going on?'

Michel dragged his eyes away from the game. 'Oh dear. I think trouble.'

Following the shifting mass was a wave of black-clad people. Police.

Then Michel laughed. 'They move the Stéphanois away from the Lyonnais. They start to fight at the corner.'

There was a different feel about the stadium now, a tense excitement. The match went on, and I began to understand what was going on.

A St Etienne player fell dramatically and lay on his face for several seconds on the bright grass. The referee came over, walked away, and a derisive chant filled the place.

Michel grinned. 'He try to get sympathy, but the referee will not blow his whistle, so they do not gain any time.'

I watched. The green man lay for a few more seconds, then got up. He limped away with the whole of the Lyonnais fans laughing and chanting.

'Suppose he's really hurt!' I said.

But he'd made his point, and when he thought no one was looking, melted back into the game with no sign of injury.

Now I was getting really interested, and when the Lyonnais team came up our end again I rose with the rest, trying to see better, cheering them on.

Another goal for us! I jumped and yelled and waved the shreds of my blue paper.

Then it was half-time and the terrible toilets and a sandwich. I put on my spare sweater, but when the match started again I didn't need it. I was sweaty with shouting and jumping up and down and laughing at our goalkeeper, at our end now. He was dressed in mustard yellow and, when the play was at the other end, he danced about and played up to the crowd. Michel told me he was a Corsican. 'He is famous for doing mad things!' We cheered his contemptuous catch when St Etienne dared to kick the ball towards our goal. We roared with disappointment when, in spite of his springing efforts, a sneaky ball got past him into the net.

Two–one. The atmosphere was electric.

Somewhere over the other side of the stadium the police moved like black beetles.

Another Stéphanois desperately tried to fake another injury. A Lyonnais had a real one, and was carried off on the sinister stretcher. An ambulance slowly drove round the running track at the edge of the pitch and disappeared somewhere in the corner.

A knot of faraway people shifted uneasily. More police beetled in, and a police car followed the path of the ambulance.

There was tension on the pitch. There was tension in the stands. The joyful waves of spectators, like a great sea surge, were no more.

Over in the covered stand to the left of us, a sudden stream of people ran uphill.

Michel looked sharply over.

'More trouble with St Etienne?' I asked. Then I looked back onto the pitch where a desperate struggle for the ball was going on.

'I think no,' said Michel. He narrowed his eyes. 'These are all our supporters. I do not know why . . .' Then the police started running uphill too, and people seemed to fall into the sides, onto other people, until they were flattened in swathes like a combine harvester cutting through standing wheat.

'Some kind of real trouble!' said Michel in a fascinated, nervous whisper.

I felt a sudden curl of terror creep up my stomach. The bomber! It made sense. He hadn't been found. He could easily have travelled down from Paris to strike somewhere else. Lyon was France's second city, after all . . .

He couldn't be carrying a bomb. Not possibly. Not after all that searching. Though there had been so many people to search. Michel had told me the stadium held forty thousand people and it looked packed full to me. Forty thousand! Wouldn't it be really easy to slip past the net of *agents de sécurité* and police?

They were spoiling the match. If St Etienne got another goal . . . I really couldn't bear it. Not unless we got another one in first.

I tried to watch the match as well as the swirls of agitation over on the covered stand. Were they coming near us?

Our goalkeeper, the Corsican in mustard yellow, rushed forward to meet a challenge that I didn't even know was coming, left his goal in what looked to me a very dangerous way, and kicked the ball practically to the other side of the pitch.

'Wow! He's fantastic!' I cried and joined the crowd round us in a standing ovation.

And then there was a sudden rush through the standing people. Someone pounded the plastic seats behind me. I looked back – as did everyone else. Some people put their arms out to stop him. Others pushed them away, trying to save him.

I saw his face suddenly right next to mine, gasping for breath, sweating as much as any footballer, but with his eyes wide with fear. I recognized his face. It had been in the papers. Mum and Dad were talking about him only this morning. Just a person. Like me. Like Michel. A person who minded so much about something unfair that he had planted a bomb to make his point.

One person, with all those police after him. It didn't seem fair, even if he might kill people with his bombs. If people listened to him instead . . .

He had reached the gangway – not much room there. It was full of people sitting on the steps. They'd never allow that in England, I found myself thinking crazily. And the police came running along our seats, running, running.

I sat down.

Michel, with a startled look round, sat too.

Most of the people in our row sat, then the people behind, following each other just as they had when they rose to clap a goal.

And the police had to get off the seats to push their way past our knees, trampling on bags, kicking shins.

I sort of saw him, fighting his way to the top, with the police wading through people after him.

But then there was a roar from the crowd, and I had to look towards the pitch.

All was quiet behind us, nothing more happened to disturb the match.

I forgot the bomber, and gripped Michel's arm as we went into injury time. People kept turning their heads to look at the great clock behind us.

I nearly screamed when the ball came close to our goal; really screamed when it went the other end.

And at last, the relief. It was the end, and we had won!

I had forgotten the bomber, as I said, until we tried to get out. The message came down from the top: the police weren't letting anyone out just yet.

But the singing had started already. Voices, already hoarse, roared songs of victory and insult. And at last we could go, though the St Etienne supporters would have to wait a bit longer.

From the top of the stand, waiting to get out of the gates, it was like a volcanic eruption – people moving in the slow heat of victory like a lava flow down the street.

'I wonder if he got away,' said Michel.

'I don't know,' I said. 'I suppose he should be punished, really. Do you think someone might listen to what he has to say, though?'

'Who knows?' said Michel, but his shrug suggested that he didn't think it was very likely.

We had to walk all the way home: there weren't any more buses going in our direction. Cheerfully we marched with the cars, singing the victory song, klaxons hooting the victory rhythm, windows open in the apartments we passed and people looking out, knowing that Lyon had won.

The lights were still on in the flat when we reached home.

'We've just seen it on the news!' said Dad. He gave me a surprisingly fierce hug.

'Yeah! We won!' I cried with satisfaction.

'That man who did the bombing. They showed us

the struggle outside the stadium. Are you all right?'
Mum was pale with anxiety.

'Of course I'm all right,' I said, emerging from her
suffocating embrace. 'It didn't spoil the match, at least
only for a little bit.'

Michel's French was far too fast for us to follow.
His father would translate for Mum and Dad later.
The police had had a tip-off that the bomber might
be at the match, Michel's father said. Mum wasn't
really reassured that the security had been very good,
and that if he had been carrying a gun or a bomb they
would have found it. She kept on looking at me as if
to make sure I was still around.

I had to remember to buy a paper at the airport
tomorrow. There'd be some really good pictures, with
any luck, to show my friends.

Of the bomber? Well, I supposed there'd be that,
too. But what I wanted was a picture of my favourite
goalkeeper, doing a flying save!

Will I ever go to a football match again?

Try and stop me!

Jennings Uses His Head

Anthony Buckeridge

(From *Jennings Goes to School*)

Jennings spent most of Saturday morning with his fingers crossed. So many obstacles had arisen to block his path to the Second Eleven, that he could hardly believe that they had been successfully overcome. Now, however, with bilious attacks and detentions safely behind him, there was nothing to stop him from realizing his ambition. All the same, he was on his guard lest fate should intervene with another cruel blow.

His usual method of going down to breakfast was to take the stairs two at a time, and the last three in one enormous leap, but today he walked sedately, grasping the banisters firmly in case a chance slip should result in a sprained ankle. Carefully he scanned the faces at the breakfast table, in case some wretched creature had come out in spots during the night and it would be Linbury's turn to telephone messages of cancellation. However, everyone's complexion seemed as flawless as could be expected, and Jennings breathed again.

At two-thirty, two taxis turned into the school drive, and the Bracebridge team arrived, accompanied by an apologetic Mr Parkinson.

'I'm most terribly sorry for that stupid mistake about the quarantine,' he said, as Mr Carter greeted him. 'It must have put you to considerable inconvenience.'

'That's quite all right,' Mr Carter assured him. 'It didn't cause us any trouble, did it, Wilkins?' He turned to his colleague for confirmation.

'Eh? Oh, no, no, no, not at all,' Mr Wilkins replied hastily, avoiding Mr Carter's eye.

The home team was already on the pitch, wearing quartered shirts of magenta and white. In honour of the occasion, Jennings had washed the back of his knees as well as the front, and had obtained some new white laces which he had twisted under and over and round his boots in a cat's cradle of complex design. He then tied two knots on top of the bow for safety, and a third one for luck. The youngest member of the team was ready for the fray!

As soon as the visitors had changed, they streamed out on the field and Mr Carter, in shorts and blazer, blew his whistle and the game began.

It was soon obvious that the teams were evenly matched, but to start with both sides were keyed up, with their nerves sharpened by the importance of the occasion. As a result, the standard of play suffered, for an excited atmosphere breeds wasteful energy rather than careful play. During the first ten minutes both goals were bombarded with shots, some lucky, some wildly impossible. Gradually, however, their nerves were steadied and their play improved: tactics and skill replaced brute force and ignorance. In fifteen minutes, they had settled down to concentrate on control of the ball, and combination of movement.

The teams played in silence, while the spectators on the touchline shouted encouragement.

'Linbury!' they yelled, in rolling waves of sound, and held on to the last note of their cry until their breath gave out. 'Linbury! Come on, Linbury!'

Loudest of all the school supporters was Mr Wilkins. It was as though he kept an amplifier in his throat for these important occasions, and as he swept up and down the touchline, his tremendous encouragement surged out across the pitch so that the players had difficulty in hearing the referee's whistle.

In contrast to this, Bracebridge had only the thin and reedy tones of Mr Parkinson to urge them on, and his voice was as the soft sighing of the west wind compared with Mr Wilkins' stentorian north-easterly gale.

The only other supporter for Bracebridge was their linesman who, owing to his role, should really have been impartial, but he was an opportunist, and carefully waited for the lulls between the shouts for Linbury to squeak, 'Play up, Bracebridge!' at the top of his voice.

The play swept from one goal mouth to the other. Now, the Bracebridge forwards had the ball and were attacking strongly. A long, low, swerving shot came in from the left wing and Parslow, in goal for Linbury, dived to make a brilliant save. The school clapped and cheered and smacked each other on the back, and Mr Wilkins switched on his loud-hailer at full volume.

'Good save,' he boomed. 'Jolly well done!'

The ball was cleared and away went the Linbury forwards, Temple, at outside-left, streaking down the field with the ball at his toes. A moment later he, too, had made a long, low, swerving shot and it was the Bracebridge goalkeeper's turn to dive and gather the ball safely to his chest before kicking it clear.

Linbury clapped the goalkeeper dutifully while their faces registered disappointment, and Mr Wilkins reduced the volume-control to halfway for his congratulations to the opposing goalkeeper.

The headmaster, perched on his shooting-stick, looked down the line of spectators to make sure that none had committed the fault of failing to applaud his opponents.

All through the first half the battle raged evenly and neither side scored. Jennings was playing a hard game, but he knew that he was not playing his best. As it was his first match and he was so much younger than the rest of the side, his sense of nervousness would not wear off. Desperately he sought to make up in energy what he felt was lacking in control.

His first chance came in the second half – and he missed it!

Linbury were attacking, and a pass came to him from the left wing. The goalkeeper was out of position and Jennings, with the ball coming straight towards him, was unmarked, less than ten yards from the goal. Even Darbishire could not have missed such an easy shot, and had Jennings been content to direct the ball gently into the net he would have scored.

But the sight of the open goal filled him with a desire to drive the ball with net-severing force. He drew back his right foot, swung it forward with all his might – and missed the ball completely!

Johnson was just behind him, cool-headed and capable, and avoiding the floundering Jennings, he trapped the ball dead and casually propelled it into the net.

The whistle blew: one–nil.

The crowd on the touchline went wild with delight

while Mr Wilkins, as excited as the youngest of them, shouted, 'Goal! Jolly good shot!' with such volume that Mr Parkinson, who was standing near by, decided to watch the rest of the match from the other side of the pitch. He departed, gently massaging his ear to relieve the air-pressure on his eardrum.

Jennings walked up the field feeling very small. It was satisfying to be one goal up, but it was maddening that he, who should have scored so easily, should have thrown away his chance and left the capable Johnson to put the damage right. He tried hard to make up for his lapse and for the next few minutes he played an inspired game.

'Well, I'm doing all right now, anyway,' he told himself, and then he proceeded to make his second unforgivable blunder.

The Bracebridge forwards were pressing hard now, eager to level the score, and Jennings dropped back to his own penalty area.

'Get up the field,' Johnson told him. 'You're miles out of position.'

Jennings took no notice: he would show them how well he could save a desperate situation, and no one could blame him for being slightly out of place if he stopped the other side from scoring.

He was standing by the side of the goalkeeper when the Bracebridge centre-half kicked the ball towards the goal. It was never meant to be a shot, and it was not even a good pass, for the ball bounced slowly towards the goalkeeper, and Parslow would have had no difficulty in catching it waist high, and clearing to the wing. He was already cupping his arms to take the ball when Jennings leapt in front of him and attempted a clearance kick.

He was not quite quick enough, however, for instead of taking the ball fairly on his instep, it glanced off the side of his boot and was deflected in a wide curve into the corner of the net.

The whistle blew: one–all.

The groan that rose to the lips of the spectators was silenced by the headmaster's reproving stare, and, as in duty bound, a tepid clapping of gloved hands was just audible above the delighted squeaks of the Bracebridge linesman.

'Why do we have to clap when we're sorry, sir?' Atkinson asked Mr Wilkins.

'You're applauding your opponents' good play,' was the reply.

'But it wasn't good play, sir. Their chap didn't even mean to shoot, did he, sir? It was Jennings who scored, wasn't it, sir?'

'Yes, I suppose it was, really.'

'Well, why do we have to clap then, sir?'

'Because . . . Oh, watch the game,' said Mr Wilkins.

Jennings had never felt so unhappy in his life. It was an accident certainly, but a stupid, clumsy sort of accident that would never have happened if he had kept his place and not tried to interfere.

Nobody said anything, but their silence was so eloquent that he squirmed with embarrassment as he took his place for the re-start of the game. Both sides were playing grimly now; there were only a few minutes to go and the level score urged them to play as though their lives depended on it.

On the touchline Darbishire, with notebook in hand, was wondering what to write next. As self-appointed sports reporter, he wanted to give his friend a good press notice, but it was straining the bonds of friendship to have to lavish praise on one who was so obviously responsible for disaster.

He consulted Atkinson and showed him what he had written:

On the last Saturday of term, Atkinson read, *a massive crowd gathered on the touchline to witness a gargantuan struggle when we played Bracebridge School in the Royal and Ancient Sport of Kings as it is called known as Association football better known as soccer. They won the toss and chose to play down the inkline although it is not much of a one and you can hardly call it a slope.*

'It's all right up to there,' said the press correspondent, 'but in the next para. I call Jennings the doughty pivot of the team. Here, look, just after this bit about the ball being literally glued to his flashing feet.'

'What's a doughty pivot?' demanded Atkinson.

'I'm not sure,' Darbishire replied, 'but I got it out of a newspaper, so it's bound to be a really stylish way of saying he's good, and now he's gone and made that frantic bish and scored a goal against us.'

'Well, why not leave out all that about the glue on his feet and say that Jennings would have been a pivot if he hadn't made a bish. Benedick's looking at his watch. It must be nearly time.'

'Yes, I suppose I... Wow, what's happening?' Darbishire looked up as the cheers of the spectators rose to a roar, for in the last minute of the game Jennings had found his form.

Intercepting an opponent's pass, he was off down the field, dribbling the ball so brilliantly that Darbishire's reference to his flashing feet seemed almost credible.

He swerved right and left through the Bracebridge forward line and left the attacking half-backs standing helpless and defeated. The Linbury forwards sprinted down the field in his wake, but they had been hanging back and Jennings was now a good twenty yards ahead of his colleagues. With a deft flick, he pushed the ball round the Bracebridge full back and was away again with only the goalkeeper to beat. For a moment the goalkeeper hesitated, started to rush out, changed his mind and retreated between the posts.

Jennings bore down upon him, every line of his body expressing determination. In the fifty-ninth minute of the eleventh hour his chance had come. One sure, swift shot and he would have made atonement for his disastrous mistake.

The touchline seethed with excitement, but Jennings was oblivious to everything except the ball at his feet, and the agitated goalkeeper ahead. He steadied himself and drew back his foot for the shot of a life-time. He could not miss.

He could!

The goal was seven feet high by twenty-one feet wide; the goalkeeper was four and a half feet high and one foot wide. It was a pity that, with nearly one hundred and fifty square feet of goal-mouth yawning like a cavern before him, Jennings had to direct his shot straight at the small figure hopping nervously in the middle of the goal.

The goalkeeper cannot be said to have saved the shot, for he was too agitated to be capable of skilful movement, but his presence on the goal line was sufficient. The ball hit him fairly on the right knee and soared upwards and over the bar.

Jennings did not hear the groans of the spectators.

He stood stock-still, unable to believe his eyes, but the damage was done, and the whistle had sounded for a corner kick.

Why, oh, why, did he have to go and throw away the chance of a lifetime? He could have kicked himself. Now, of course, there would be no time to make good the damage, for Mr Carter was looking at his watch and would blow the final whistle immediately after the corner kick had been taken. There was nothing more to be done; he had had every chance to justify his place in the team, and he had failed.

A despairing silence gripped the spectators as Nuttall, on the right wing, prepared to take the corner kick.

Darbishire put away his notebook and looked up to watch the last kick being taken.

He caught sight of Jennings, and his heart was wrung by his friend's expression of woe. Unmindful of the fact that you do not cheer when the ball is out of play, he suddenly broke the silence by shouting:

'Never mind, Jennings. Better luck next time!'

Nuttall was just running up to take the kick when Darbishire shouted, and, at the sound of his name, Jennings turned his head for a split second towards the spectators on the left touchline.

Thus it was that he did not see the ball hurtling towards his head until it was too late. Out of the corner of his eye, he saw an object about to hit him and, without stopping to think, he jumped to avoid it. His instinct, however, betrayed him, and instead of flinching away from the missile, he jumped right into the trajectory of its flight. With a thud, the ball hit him squarely in the middle of his forehead and knocked him off his feet.

He lay on the ground for a moment with his eyes shut, while he recovered from the shock. Thus he did not see the Bracebridge goalkeeper picking the ball from the back of the net; he did not hear Mr Carter blow his whistle to indicate a goal, and immediately afterwards blow a long, final blast as the signal that the game was over; he was unconscious of the stampede of delight which swept along the touchline, as sixty-eight pairs of Wellington boots executed an ungainly war-dance, while an equal number of vocal chords vied with one another in building up a roaring cataract of cheers.

The first thing Jennings knew was that the entire Second Eleven were helping him to his feet and patting him on the back.

'Fantastically well done, Jennings,' said Nuttall, pounding him heavily between the shoulder blades. 'A real smasher.'

Jennings blinked uncertainly at the ring of smiling faces around him. What on earth were they feeling so pleased about?

'Finest header I've ever seen,' said Brown. 'The way you leapt at it and then, *wham*! – right into the top corner of the net.'

'And the force of it, too!' added Johnson. 'You must have put all your weight behind it or you wouldn't have gone down flat like that, after you'd whammed it in.'

It took Jennings a few seconds to grasp the signifi-cance of these remarks. So they had won the match after all, and it was due to his alleged header in the final second! Well, it was very gratifying, of course, to be acclaimed as the hero of the hour, but what would they say if they knew that his wonder goal was the accidental result of the most frightful bish in the history of soccer?

'Well,' he said hesitantly, 'it's terrifically nice of you all to be so decent about it, but ...' The temptation to bask in unearned glory was strong, but virtuously he decided to tell the truth. 'As a matter of fact, the whole thing was just a fluke.'

Cries of protest greeted this statement.

'Go and boil yourself,' they said affectionately. 'You can't fool us like that.'

It was all very well to be modest and self-effacing, but Jennings was surely entitled to take the credit for his spectacular shot.

'It was a goal in a thousand,' said Temple admiringly.

'Nonsense!' said Jennings.

'Well, a goal in a hundred, then.'

'Oh no,' said Jennings.

'Well, anyway, it was a goal,' Temple amended.

'Oh, well,' said Jennings. If they wouldn't believe it was an accident, what more could he say?

Happily, the team escorted their visitors off the pitch.

'There's one thing about old Jennings,' Brown said to Johnson, as he splashed in the kneebath some ten minutes later. 'He doesn't swank as much as he used to. The way he back-pedalled about that terrific header of his: anyone who didn't know, might really think it had been a fluke after all.'

'Yes,' agreed Johnson, 'he certainly knows how to use his head.'

Stickers

Dave Ward

Miss Pringle's voice was shrill as a referee's whistle.

'I don't want to see them any more. You've all gone football mad and it's just got to stop.'

She waved a fistful of footy stickers in front of the rows of crestfallen faces lined up in the hall for school assembly. Terry was sitting at the back, an action replay going through his head of missing a sitter in last Sunday's match. Maybe what Paul Bryant had said was true – he was better at sticking stickers in his album than sticking the ball in the back of the net. So now he could hardly bear to listen to what Miss Pringle was saying.

'If you paid as much attention to your teachers as you did to swapping these bits of card, we might finish a little higher in the *education* league tables. So I don't want to see them any more. Not in class, not at playtime, not at dinnertime . . . Paul Bryant, what's that you've got behind your back? I hope it's not what I think. Bring them out here at once!'

Terry watched Paul shuffle up to the front. Paul was the boss of Terry's team, the Tornadoes, but his last transfer deal was over – his fistful of prize stars confiscated, to be stuck on top of Miss Pringle's cupboard. Game over until the end of the season. Or so Miss Pringle thought.

But the next morning, same as ever, Terry and his mates gathered outside the newsagent's, clutching wodges of football pictures. While their dads frowned over the number of noughts in the latest transfer deals on the back pages of the papers, Terry's mates were haggling over more important transactions, as they hoarded their precious cards.

'I'll swap you that for this one, Terry.'

'No way. That one's not on swaps.'

'I'll give you two.'

'*I'll* give you three.'

'*I'll* give you this whole team.' Terry could never figure out why you'd get loads of some players when others hardly came up at all in those brightly wrapped packs of bubble gum. The ones everyone wanted were always hardest to get, especially the leading scorers in their own local Premier League team.

Cedric had a theory; he always did.

'Maybe the manufacturers make sure only a few Liverpool players are in the packs that go to the Liverpool shops, or only a few Newcastle players get sent to Newcastle. That way we have to keep on buying them, just to get the ones we want.'

Cedric peeled back the wrapper on his latest purchase.

'Aw, I've got all these,' he exclaimed, detaching them from the bubble gum which he dumped straight into the bin. The bubble gum was dread – it turned your tongue bright green. Paul Bryant swallowed some once and felt so sick he nearly missed out on their next match in the Sunday Youth League.

After school the swaps went on, by the treehouse down in the park. Miss Pringle hadn't stopped them at all. They just hid the stickers safely away through the day, deep inside pockets, coat linings and socks – whispering deals at playtime and at the back of the school dinner queue.

'Tony's got Coventry's striker.'

'Tell him I'll see him later. That'll do me fine to get the whole team.'

And the whole team was just what was desperately needed, because up in the treehouse another deal was going down.

The young team bosses were jabbering away. They were each in charge of a team their own age, for the Youth Association's Sunday League. They had their own coaches and trainers too, to show they could learn every part of the game and not just the skills on the pitch. But it was skills on the pitch that concerned them now.

'You can have Ritcho for the whole Tottenham team.'

'What about Arsenal?'

'Nah. It's got to be Spurs. He's worth it – you know he is. Look at him go.'

From their spyhole in the treehouse, the team bosses could get a bird's eye view. And they whistled in appreciation as Ritcho set off on a dazzling run.

Ritcho was the boy with it all. He was tall, good-looking (or so the girls said), with a change of speed and ball control that left defenders dead.

'He's brilliant!'

'Ball greedy, you mean.'

Ritcho wasn't bothered with the rest of the team – he could do it all on his own. The ball flew straight between the piles of stacked-up coats marking out the goal.

Ritcho was a match-winner – head and shoulders

above the rest in every sense. He was nearly a foot taller than everyone else. On Sundays when they played their League games he had to bring his birth certificate with him because visiting teams would never believe his age.

He could header balls without jumping. He could dribble and twist like a snake. Terry tried tackling him once. It wasn't that Ritcho went round him, or powered straight through – it was the way he made Terry feel as if he wasn't even there!

He had his own band of travelling fans who screamed with joy at his handstands every time he scored a goal. And screamed even more at the victory raps he made up right there on the spot, then repeated like an action replay each week at Stealers, the disco club that all the big kids went to – with the same swivelling hips, ducks and dips that had so devastatingly shaken off opposing defenders.

Yes, Ritcho was a star. The trouble was, sometimes he behaved like one, too. He never turned up for training but, like he said, it didn't really matter because he always played so well. *'Just get the ball to Ritcho and he'll stick it in the net'* were all the tactics needed when Ritcho was on your team. And whichever team he played for always seemed to win.

But Ritcho never played for any team for too long. Everyone was always keen to sign him, then just as keen to pass him on. There were lots of different reasons muttered round the playground. Sometimes other players got jealous. Sometimes they got fed up with his gang of fans turning up at training, even when he himself didn't. Sometimes they said he was impossibly big-headed. But they never complained when he put the ball in the net.

His wages were the biggest problem. Rumours started to spread. Ritcho wanted six footy stickers just to turn out on the pitch, and three more for every goal he scored. And then it was five. Soon he started demanding complete team sets with managers and kits – even whole albums.

Was he worth it? some started asking. But the answer always came back, *yes*. Because if there was one thing you could bank on – whichever team Ritcho played for would always win the match. If he stayed long enough with any one team they'd be bound to win the Sunday Youth League. But Ritcho moved on from one to another so it ended up pretty well fair. Whoever got him at the end of the season would have the edge in that final run-in. But most crucial of all was who signed him on for the Youth Association Knockout Cup.

Terry knew his own team, the Tornadoes, were desperate. Ritcho had never played for them. They knew his reputation, but they reckoned they could cope with him. After all, they hadn't got much to lose. In fact, they'd lost nearly every game they'd played: mostly to goals by Ritcho, turning out for one team after another in a succession of different shirts. And he always looked great as well – whichever shirt he wore was always pressed and neat, his socks never slipped, and his boots were bright and clean.

One afternoon he even played for two teams – one match after another without pausing for breath. It was effortless. In fact, in the second game he scored a bucketful of goals then just strolled off before the final whistle.

'Send a sub on – there's no way they'll catch you now,' he'd grinned. 'I'm off to get a shower, get home and changed then out to the disco. *Two* victory raps to knock out tonight. And it'll be a knockout all right.'

Terry had watched him, open mouthed. He was even signing autographs at the door of the changing room.

So Terry's team just *had* to sign up Ritcho. Their manager had sent out an SOS for everyone to pool every sticker, every album, everything they'd got to clinch the transfer deal. Terry was rummaging under his bed. His album was nearly full. He fished around for stray stickers to see if he could complete the league. Just then his grandad came into the room.

'What're you looking for, son?'

Terry proudly showed his grandad the album, every player stuck neatly in place.

'You're just as bad as I was.' His grandad shook his head, disappeared for a few minutes and then returned, blowing the dust off a heavily bound book. He opened the pages with satisfaction, showing them off to Terry. Rows of ancient faces stared right back at him. Famous names his grandad recited: Johnnie Haynes, Dannie Blanchflower . . . Lines of neat partings, knotted arms and firm-set chins.

'Those were the days, son, when footballers looked like footballers – not pin-ups or pop stars or models. And they played like footballers too, with none of your fancy wages. The game's just getting too greedy. I don't know where it'll end.'

Terry always ignored his grandad's remarks – he was sure all the singers and film stars looked that way then as well. But he seized the album excitedly. Every page seemed to tell a story – all the great teams of the past, labelled in his grandad's rounded schoolboy lettering.

Terry could tell his grandad had spent ages building up every team and pasting them carefully into their places.

'Oh, Grandad – can I take this with me, just to show all my mates? They'd be amazed to see it, really. Especially Cedric – he probably even knows all the players' names.'

Cedric knew everything about football. He probably even knew how many goals those old players had scored and what season they made their debut.

Terry's grandad hesitated.

'I don't know – you'll have to be careful. This album goes way back – every page is like a memory.'

Terry's face was a picture of pleading.

'Well, all right, I suppose there's no harm showing your mates what *real* footballers looked like. But watch you don't lose it or bend it. That's a real piece of history you've got there.'

Terry wrapped the album in a clean towel and placed it in a carrier bag alongside his own collection, which looked dog-eared and tatty now.

Down at the treehouse Terry unwrapped the album. His mates all clustered round as if they'd discovered a treasure. They sighed and exclaimed and turned the pages on a journey back in time. Cedric explained all the dates and the records, just like Terry knew he would.

'So anyway,' said Terry finally, 'here's my own album.' He fished it out of his bag. 'We need all we can get if we're going to sign Ritcho for the Cup.'

But their junior manager just squinted at it briefly from under the peak of his baseball cap. He ran his fingers longingly over the gold embossed binding and heavy reinforced pages of the old football album.

'Terry – *this* is what we need. Never mind all that other stuff. We'd have Ritcho on a permanent contract if we could just use this.'

'But it isn't mine, it's Grandad's,' Terry muttered.

'Oh, go on – he won't miss it. Look at the dust on the cover. Your grandad hasn't looked at it for years. I bet it's been stuck in a cupboard, like all of our stickers Miss Pringle's got. At least this way it's doing some good.'

'Just think,' Cedric chimed in, 'one day Ritcho might be in a book like this – and it'll say he started with us!'

Terry couldn't believe the look on his dad's face.

'*You did what?*' he roared. 'You know that album was your grandad's pride and joy. I used to sit and look at it myself when I was a boy. And now you've gone and given it away!'

Terry didn't know what to say. He tried to find the words to explain how much it meant to his team to sign Ritcho, and how much they needed the album. But he knew his dad wouldn't see it that way.

'You'll just have to swap it back before Grandad finds out, that's all!'

So Terry set out with a bag full of swag – all the stickers he could muster, even 3D frames, programmes and scarves. Anything he could lay his hands on to get his grandad's album back. He knew it wouldn't be easy, but the least he could do was try.

He found Ritcho's ex-manager down in the tree-house as he knew he would. Terry spilled his offerings across the rough plank floor, grabbing the scarf so it didn't snag on any nails.

'What's all this then?'

'My grandad's album – the old one, the one we gave you for Ritcho? I need it back. Well – my dad does, otherwise I reckon he'll kill me. You can have all this, but *please* give it back.'

The manager riffled through the stickers, then leant back and cracked his knuckles.

'You've got some good gear here. And I'd help you if I could. But that old album – I've traded it on. No one wants cards and stickers any more, especially not Ritcho. Anyway, I'm trying to set up another deal to get him to come back to us. This is what he's after now.'

The manager spread out a set of team posters to show Terry the score. Out on the field Ritcho was flexing and weaving, going through his paces, leaving them all for dead without even breaking sweat.

Terry turned white, then red.

'So who's got the album now? It's not yours, it's not mine, it's my grandad's. I've *got* to get it back.'

The manager scratched his head. 'I tell you what,' he said in the end. 'Give me your stickers and I'll let you have these posters. Take them over and see the Wanderers. That's where the album is now.'

Terry set off with the posters under his arm, on the long walk to the other side of town. Past the chip shop, by the brewery and over the old canal, till he came to where the Wanderers hid out, round the back of the bus depot.

Terry held his breath. There was a reek of dust and diesel fumes as he crept along the fence. A gang of

Wanderers' sharpshooters were slamming a ball with accuracy at a target on the wall.

'Look who it is.'

'It's that Terry kid.'

'What're you doing over this way, lad? Sure you know your way home?'

Terry tried to roll the posters out, but the wind made them flap and bend.

'I've got to get Grandad's album back,' he tried his best to explain.

'But we haven't got your grandad's album,' said the Wanderers' captain. 'We swapped it for all these pop posters.' He pulled them out of his kit bag. 'It was our manager that got them. I think he wants to do some deal to try and sign Ritcho for our team. Reckons Ritcho's seriously into music so these posters might do the trick.'

'What am I going to do now? What's my dad going to say?' Terry looked around anxiously. It was starting to get dark.

The Wanderers' captain shrugged and tucked the pop posters under Terry's arm.

'You can have them if you want. I'm not that bothered anyway – and I think the deal with Ritcho fell through.'

Terry trudged home thoughtfully. The last thing his grandad would want would be this clutch of pin-ups and pop stars. And sadly he realized he hadn't even got his *own* stickers any more.

Next day he found out that his own team had already lost Ritcho. Terry had sacrificed his own collection and his grandad's too – and his manager had gone and swapped their one star player for a pile of designer T-shirts.

'Honest, Terry, there was nothing I could do,' the manager explained as they sat round in the treehouse. 'It was what Ritcho wanted. He said we were no good and he was leaving anyway, so I thought the best I could do was get six T-shirts out of it.'

'Six T-shirts. Where's the other three?' Terry could see the manager and his two mates were wearing one each.

'Ritcho's got them. That was what he wanted – his signing-on fee for the Express.'

The Express. So that's where Ritcho had ended up. It didn't seem right at all. They'd probably win the Cup anyway, whether they'd got Ritcho or not. They'd got all the other best players, the best kit, the best sponsors – the lot. And no doubt Ritcho had a rap ready-made. 'Express Yourself', or something like that. Terry could see him now, posing on the mike at the disco.

But most important of all, he still had to get his grandad's album back.

'Give me the T-shirts,' he insisted, and made the manager and his sidekicks peel them off, right then and there in the treehouse.

Terry arrived at the Final late. The designer T-shirts were neatly ironed and stashed away in his bag. It had taken him ages to get them done: he kept trying to avoid his mum in case she asked awkward questions. And his dad just hadn't spoken to him for what felt like days on end.

'What's the score?' he asked someone casually,

assuming that Ritcho and the Express would have knocked up a cricket total by now.

'Wanderers are winning three–one.'

It took a moment to sink in. Terry's eyes scanned the length of the field. Ritcho wasn't there. Express still had eleven players, so he couldn't have been sent off.

'Did Ritcho get injured?'

'No, mate. He isn't playing.'

It was true. Terry suddenly realized that Ritcho's huddle of travelling fans were nowhere to be seen either.

Puzzled and suddenly bold, he marched straight up to the Express's junior manager.

'Where's Ritcho then?'

'I wish I knew. Well, in fact I do. He never showed. Just sent a message saying he'd gone into town. Something about a talent contest – they're auditioning this morning. He's gone to show off his raps – and I bet he's wearing one of those flash designer T-shirts we got him as a signing-on fee.'

'You mean one like these?'

Terry unzipped his bag.

The manager nodded.

'Well, listen,' Terry insisted. 'I want you to take them back. And I want *you* to give *me* my grandad's football album . . .'

Just at that moment the Wanderers' captain scored another goal to put the match well and truly out of reach of the Express.

Their manager opened his kitbag.

'You mean *this*?' He pulled the album out. 'You can take it, mate. You can keep the shirts. I'm sick of it all. I don't want to see them any more.'

'That's funny,' said Cedric, who'd suddenly appeared at Terry's side. 'That's just what Miss Pringle said.'

But then, thought Terry, Cedric had to come up with some clever remark. He always did, did Cedric.

Gary's Goal

Alan Durant

Gary Connor had a lot to live up to – at least, he felt he had.

Well, there was his name for a start. His dad, Charlie Connor, had been a lifelong Leicester City supporter and had named his younger son after his favourite player, Gary Lineker – even though by the time Gary had been born, the super striker had long since moved on to new and more glamorous pastures.

Then there was his dad himself. A talented footballer, Charlie Connor was a legend in his home town, having been the star of the local non-league team, Mossington Borough. When people talked about him their eyes filled with warmth and admiration – and sadness too, for Charlie Connor had been killed, tragically, in a road accident two years ago, when Gary was ten.

Gary's mum was still grieving. She tried to put on a brave face, but Gary had often heard her weeping in her room at night. Recently, though, she'd got some consolation from the footballing progress of Gary's older brother, Steve, who, at fifteen, had started to play regularly for Mossington Borough. He was beginning to attract the interest of some big clubs, too, and just a couple of weeks ago Leicester City had offered him a trial. But then misfortune had struck. In attempting to score a goal, Steve had collided with a defender and fractured his left leg. He was expected to be out of football for at least six months. A heavy gloom had descended on the family once more – and it seemed to Gary that only he could lift it.

Gary was no mean footballer himself. He was a prolific goalscorer for his school team and had just joined the Junior football side, St Jude's, that his brother had played in for several years. Much was expected of him; indeed, he expected much of himself.

He was the youngest player in the team and, as yet, he didn't feel entirely at ease with his team-mates. They all seemed to know each other well and, though his first couple of games had gone OK, he still felt a bit of an outsider. A goal, he thought, would make all the difference. Once he'd scored, then he'd be more confident and his team-mates would really accept him as part of the team. Yes, a goal was all he needed.

A couple more games went by, though, without him scoring. He hit the post, hit the bar, the goalies made brilliant saves, he had a header cleared off the line . . . He did everything but score that elusive first goal. He was playing well and the rest of the team were scoring, however, so no one seemed particularly concerned about his lack of goals – except Gary, of course. He thought about it all the time. It became a complete obsession: scoring was quite literally his goal.

In the games that followed, an air of desperation hung over his play. He would shoot from anywhere, any angle . . . But the harder he tried to score, the wilder his attempts became. He'd balloon shots way over the bar or metres wide of the post; even when he got an easy chance, he'd fluff it. Once he sliced the ball past the post from inside the six-yard box with the goalie nowhere near. It was the openest of open goals and he missed it. He went home from that match feeling like a total failure.

He didn't show it, though. He didn't want his mum or his brother to think there was anything wrong. They had more than enough to deal with already. So when his mum asked him how it went, Gary forced a smile. 'Fine,' he said lightly. 'We won.'

'How many did you get?' Steve asked, jokily.

'Oh, I didn't score,' Gary shrugged. 'But the team got three. That's all that matters.'

'Yeah, well said,' his brother agreed. Then he pulled a face. 'I wish you'd tell that to some of my team-mates,' he said.

On the morning of Gary's next match, Steve surprised him by announcing that he was going to watch.

'What about your leg?' Gary asked.

'I've got my crutches,' Steve said. 'It'll be good exercise for me. Besides, it'll be fun to see my old team. Who knows, maybe I'll learn a thing or two.' He grinned at Gary. Steve was always so good-humoured, Gary thought. He never seemed to get really down. He appeared to be able to cope with anything – losing a dad, breaking a leg . . . If only I were like that, Gary thought.

Having his brother at the game as a spectator made Gary even more desperate than ever to achieve his goal. This match against Paynes Park had to be the one. Today, he just *had* to score.

At the kick-off, he looked across towards the touchline and saw Steve standing next to the St Jude's coach, Matthew Harvey. Steve grinned and gave his younger brother a big thumbs-up.

'Come on, St Jude's!' he shouted.

Despite his brother's encouragement, things didn't go well for Gary. In the first half, he struggled to get into the match. The few times he got the ball within shooting range of the Paynes Park goal, he wasted the opportunities – either by losing control of the ball or by blasting it well wide. Even the most basic skills seemed to be beyond him: he made a mess of trapping the ball and his passing was hopelessly inaccurate. He could sense the growing frustration and impatience of his team-mates.

'You OK, Gary?' Steve asked him at half-time.

'Yeah,' Gary said, with a swagger he didn't feel. He shook his head. 'The pitch is really bobbly.' He glanced across nervously at Matthew Harvey, afraid that the coach might substitute him for the second half since he had been so awful in the first.

During the interval, Gary kept as close to his brother as possible, hoping that somehow this might save him. But when Danny Swan, the reserve, took off his track-suit, Gary feared the worst. Then his tense eyes caught sight of Nathan Martin hobbling off the pitch, and he sighed with relief. He was still in the match.

The relief was only temporary, though. As soon as the second half began, he was once more weighed down by the pressure to get a goal, and Steve's cries of encouragement just made it worse. Gary couldn't let him down. It wasn't just Steve either – it was Mum, it was Dad, it was the whole family. He *had* to deliver.

If the first half had been like a bad dream for Gary, the second was a full-blown nightmare. He played as though he were in a game of his own. When he got the ball he went for goal, oblivious to the calls of his team-mates.

After a lacklustre first half, St Jude's were back to their best, producing some flowing football. But every move foundered when it reached Gary. Three times, he had golden opportunities to play a team-mate in for a simple tap-in, but instead he went for goal himself and, almost inevitably, lost the ball.

As if to add insult to injury, after the third occasion, with a number of St Jude's players still remonstrating furiously with Gary for his selfishness, Paynes Park broke quickly and scored. The goal was totally against the run of play, but it was enough to give the visiting team victory.

When the final whistle blew, the St Jude's team trooped off the pitch, dejected and angry. No one could even bring themselves to talk to Gary. He walked behind the others, head down, consumed with misery, unable even to look at his brother. He really did wish the ground would open and swallow him.

The changing room was unusually, eerily quiet. The atmosphere was charged with resentment, but still no one said anything to Gary. They ignored him completely, just as he had them during the game.

He got changed quickly, not bothering to shower, bundled his kit in his bag and headed for the door. He wanted to be away before Matthew Harvey appeared. He felt wretched enough without having to suffer the humiliation of a public dressing-down from the coach.

But when he opened the door, without a word of farewell given or received, he quickly saw that he was not to escape so easily. Matthew Harvey was standing there waiting for him.

'Right, Gary,' he said coolly. 'Let's go round the side, shall we, where we can be private?' He started to walk away and Gary followed him. He felt sick with trepidation at what was to follow. His legs were so heavy he could barely walk.

When they were round the side of the changing hut, the coach stopped and, putting his hands on his hips, glowered at Gary.

'You, Gary Connor, are the greediest, most selfish player I have seen in all my years of coaching,' he uttered in a voice of icy rage. 'Your performance today single-handedly lost us a game we should have won – and won comfortably.'

Gary had never seen Matthew Harvey like this. Generally he was very easy-going, like a friendly uncle. The transformation now was devastating.

'I'm tempted, sorely tempted to wash my hands of you completely,' the coach continued severely. 'This club doesn't need players like you – not on your showing today anyway. Football is a team game and that's what I run, a team. If you're not prepared to be a part of that – a contributing part, I mean – then you may as well go now and not come back. I shan't be sorry, I'll tell you. If it hadn't been for your brother being here, I'd have hoiked you off in the second half, substitute or no substitute. I'd rather play with ten men than put up with that kind of selfishness. It's an insult to the rest of the team.'

Gary couldn't bring himself to raise his eyes from the ground, worm-level – because that was the way he felt, like a worm. But Matthew Harvey demanded a response. 'What have you got to say for yourself?' he said sharply.

Gary's head was bursting, like a ball that had been pumped up and up and up and couldn't take any more without exploding. What could he say? How could he start to explain? What was the point anyway? In the end, he muttered the only words that he could find among the cluttered confusion in his brain. 'I'm sorry.'

'I should think you are,' the coach chided, though his tone had thawed a little now. 'But if you want to play for St Jude's again you will have to apologize to the rest of the team – and prove that you mean it.'

'I am sorry, really,' Gary insisted wretchedly.

'Well, if everyone's satisfied that's the case, you can sit on the bench for the next game,' said Matthew Harvey. 'A spell as substitute might do you some good.'

Gary nodded.

When the coach strode away, Gary pondered what he'd just said. The next game, he recalled, was a cup match on Wednesday evening against Fairley Athletic. His mum was coming to watch. (She worked Saturdays so she rarely got to see either of her sons play.) No doubt Steve would accompany her. Now Gary had been dropped, there'd be no point in them coming. He should have felt deep disappointment, but he didn't. Instead, he felt like a load had been lifted from his shoulders. If he wasn't on the pitch, then there was no pressure on him to score.

He headed for the back of the changing hut, hoping to get away without having to see anyone. He just wanted to be out of there. But when he rounded the corner, he was surprised to find Steve waiting for him. The older boy was sitting on a bench, crutches beside him. In his misery, Gary had forgotten about Steve.

'Hi, kid,' Steve greeted him warmly. 'Give me a hand with these crutches, can you? Then we can hobble on home together. It'll give us a chance to have a chat.'

Immediately, Gary knew that Steve had overheard his exchange with Matthew Harvey. As he helped his brother get to his feet, he blushed deeply with shame.

The walk home along the footpath by the fields usually took Gary fifteen minutes. That afternoon it took four times as long. Steve struggled along on his crutches and had to stop and rest at regular intervals. But, in truth, neither brother was in a hurry to get home.

In that hour, they talked more than they had at any time during the past two years. Prompted by Steve, Gary revealed at last the pressure and strain he was feeling. He told his brother about the goal he longed for, and his frustration at not being able to achieve it. By the time he'd finished, he was in tears.

'It's OK,' Steve soothed and he put an arm round his younger brother's shoulders, drawing him close. They stood for some time like that, in an ungainly six-legged huddle, balanced precariously on the wooden crutches. Then, at last, Gary's sobbing eased and he raised his head away from his brother. 'I wish I was like you,' he said softly.

'Like me?' Steve laughed incredulously.

'Yeah,' Gary said. 'Nothing seems to get to you. You take everything in your stride. Like now, with that leg.' He shook his head sadly. 'I'd never have coped with that like you. You're so strong.'

Steve took a step back and leant against the wooden slats of the fence. He looked down at his plastered leg, then stared out over the fields, as if searching for something beyond the long grass.

When he turned back to Gary, he said, 'People deal with things in different ways, Gary. That's what Dad used to say. His way was always to be cheerful, positive, even when things were difficult. I suppose I try to be the same.' He paused a moment then, more animatedly, continued, 'I hate this injury, you know. I hate not being able to play. It's real torture. But being miserable is not going to make it get better any quicker. I've just got to be patient.' His lips formed a half smile. 'That was something else Dad used to say.' Steve pulled himself up straight on his crutches and looked his younger brother full in the eyes. 'I reckon that's what he'd have said to you now, Gary. Be patient, you know. Play your natural game. A goal will come.'

Gary nodded. 'Yeah,' he said. He knew that what Steve said was right. Anyway, he was on the subs bench now, so he'd have to be patient, wouldn't he? Who could say when he'd get on the field again?

Over the following days, Gary got on with his life quietly and calmly. He didn't feel happy – he was still too ashamed and embarrassed – but he had an inkling that he'd touched the bottom and now he could only go up.

When he got to the ground on Wednesday evening, though, his stomach was tight with nerves at the prospect of having to face his team-mates. He was relieved that the first person he saw was Matthew Harvey. The coach gave Gary a curt nod of greeting, but his expression wasn't unfriendly.

'I wasn't sure we'd see you tonight, Gary,' he said. He nodded again, this time more appreciatively. 'I'm glad you came.' He glanced towards the changing room. 'Right, let's get this apology out of the way, shall we?'

As it turned out, facing his fellow players wasn't as bad as Gary had feared. His apology was heartfelt and the rest of the team, it seemed, recognized that – anyway, he reckoned, they were too busy thinking about the evening's match to worry about him. He sat down behind Matthew Harvey, while the coach gave his team talk. As he looked on, Gary noticed, for the first time, how nervous many of the players looked. It wasn't only him, then, who suffered that way.

Gary warmed up with the other players. When the game was ready to start, he stood next to his coach on the touchline. The few spectators who'd turned up were on the opposite side of the pitch, near the halfway line. Among them were Gary's mum and Steve. They'd insisted on coming, even though Gary wasn't playing. 'Moral support', Steve had called it.

As the players lined up for the kick-off, Gary glanced across and his mum waved. The smile on her face raised his spirits – as did the extravagant thumbs-up Steve delivered. Then the whistle blew and everyone's attention was focused on the pitch.

It was a tight match with little to choose between the two teams. St Jude's had the edge on possession, but without creating much in the way of scoring chances. The one they did have was fluffed hopelessly by Gary's replacement, Danny Swan. He usually played in midfield and was finding it hard to adjust to the striker's role.

At half-time, the score was nil–nil – and so it continued into the second half. St Jude's were well on top, but Fairley defended bravely. The game was deadlocked. Gary watched tensely beside his coach, willing his side to score. Then, with twenty minutes left, Nathan Martin fell under a heavy challenge from a Fairley defender. For the second match running, he limped from the pitch and had to be substituted. Gary was on!

'Nice and steady, son,' Matthew Harvey encouraged his young substitute, as he ran to take his place on the pitch. He went straight up front in his usual position with Danny Swan dropping back into midfield.

'Good luck, Gary,' the latter muttered as they passed one another.

'Thanks,' Gary replied.

'Go it, Gary!' a familiar voice cried from somewhere behind him. It was Steve, urging his younger brother on. Gary smiled nervously, but there was cool determination in his eyes.

With Gary in attack, St Jude's play seemed immediately to be more penetrative and threatening. His first couple of touches led to shooting opportunities that narrowly failed to produce a goal. Fairley really were under pressure now and their defending became increasingly desperate. They booted the ball out of play or aimlessly upfield, just trying to hang on. Maybe they might have done too – had luck not intervened.

Once again, St Jude's swept forward, putting together a flowing move that saw the ball go from one side of the field to the other. In the centre, Gary darted into space at the near post, hoping for a cross; but when it came, it was just too far ahead of him. The ball evaded his lunge by inches. But it didn't evade Gary's marker, standing just behind. The ball smacked against the Fairley defender's shin, bobbled up and hit Gary full in the face.

'Ah!' he gasped and he screwed up his eyes at the sudden, smarting pain. When he opened them again, he couldn't believe what he saw. The ball was in the Fairley net and his team-mates were rushing to congratulate him. He'd scored! At last! He grinned, as much with incredulity at the bizarre manner of his success as the goal itself. After all those strenuous efforts he'd made to force a goal, when it finally happened, he'd known nothing about it! It was undoubtedly the luckiest goal he'd ever score, but who cared? Certainly not his team-mates; they were cock-a-hoop with joy – and so, on the touchline, was Matthew Harvey.

As Gary trotted back to the centre, he felt light as the crisp evening air, as if nothing could ever trouble him ever again. He raised his hand in a rapturous salute to his mum and to Steve, who returned the gesture so vehemently that he almost toppled from his crutches.

'Well played, Gary!' Gary's mum called. She looked so thrilled, so obviously delighted that Gary was close to tears – tears of jubilation this time, though. Nodding in acknowledgement of her approval, he had a sudden image of his dad, standing there next to her, wearing his beloved Leicester City scarf and smiling.

St Jude's were rampant now. Having finally been breached, Fairley Athletic crumbled before the home team's irresistible football. Within minutes of his first goal, Gary scored again. This time there was nothing fortunate about his effort. A quick one-two with Danny Swan took him into the Fairley penalty area. A neat, wrongfooting sidestep and he was in on goal with only the keeper to beat. As the goalie advanced, he slotted the ball coolly into the bottom right-hand corner of the net. The game was as good as won.

Gary was on fire now. He could do no wrong. He dribbled past opponents, moved and passed cleverly – he even tackled well, which wasn't usually a strong feature of his game. As the match drew to a close, he was feeling on top of the world. His most important moment, though, was yet to come.

There were only seconds left, when St Jude's stormed forward once more, cutting through the ragged Fairley midfield and defence. The ball found its way to Gary on the right edge of the penalty area with just one defender between him and the goal. His heart raced as he realized this was his golden chance for a hat-trick. As the defender came across, Gary dodged outside him, going a little wide of the goal. The angle wasn't great, but a fast, low shot might just squeeze past the keeper at his near post . . .

As he looked up to shoot, he suddenly saw Danny Swan standing on his own in the centre of the goal, just outside the six-yard box. Gary advanced on goal. The keeper dithered. Gary drew back his foot to shoot, then flicked the ball back across the goal into the path of Danny Swan, giving his team-mate the simplest of tap-ins.

It was the final action of the game. When the ball rolled into the Fairley net the referee blew his whistle for the goal and then again for the end of the match. St Jude's had beaten Fairley Athletic three goals to nil. They were through to the next round of the cup!

As they walked from the field, Gary's team-mates were full of praise for their super sub's contribution. So too was Matthew Harvey.

'Son,' he said, clapping a large hand on Gary's shoulder, 'that was a great striker's performance – hungry but not greedy.' He smiled. Then, in a quieter voice he added, 'Your dad would have been proud. Really proud.'

Gary beamed. He'd finally achieved his goal; he'd

been accepted. He really was part of the team. And, looking across at his mum and Steve, their faces smiling back at him, he could see he'd achieved the other half of his goal too. He'd made them happy.

Gruesome Gran and the Broken Promise

Trevor Millum

The Barrow Boys played for Barrowby School. Some of us didn't actually go to the school, but we all knew someone who did. We used to practise on the playing field at the top of Mill Road – a long way from the school but the only decent pitch in the village.

It's a big village, mind you, but there's not much space in it for playing football. Cricket's even more difficult because the whole point is to slog the ball as far as you can. At least in football the general idea is to try and keep the ball on the pitch. Not that we always succeeded.

I always seemed to be the one to knock it over someone's hedge. I don't know what it is about me, but the ball hits my boots and flies off like a five year-old on a trampoline. Big Foot, the team captain, calls me Buttertoes, but I don't think that's very clever – or very accurate either. But I don't argue with him. I want to keep my place in the team.

We had a bad time last week. Well, to be honest, *I* had a bad week. We had a practice Tuesday night and it was going great. We even had Mountain Boy in goal and he's ace. He doesn't move all that fast but it's really hard to get the ball past him, and no one would dream of charging him – not even Loopy Lee, who'll do most things. He does mad things because he thinks it'll make people like him. I don't know where he got the idea from that people would love someone who does stupid things, but there you go.

Anyway, as I was saying, we had a good time trying to get the ball past Mountain Boy and I thought I was playing pretty well. I was out on the wing when Gonzo did something he hardly ever does. He passed the ball. Even more unlikely, he passed the ball to me! I trapped it, and set off towards the goal. I didn't see the need to pass to anyone else. I could just see daylight between Mountain Boy and the goalpost and I lammed it straight into the gap. At least, I thought it was straight into the gap. In fact, it looped up and flew over the top of the goal and landed in one of the gardens.

'Buttertoes!' yelled Big Foot. 'Go and get it!'

'Yeah, yeah!' I said. I knew the rules. The trouble with the houses that backed onto the playing field was that they all seemed to be occupied by people who were as mad as Loopy Lee. If they weren't mad, their dogs were.

I looked over the fence to see if there was anyone about. You were supposed to go all the way round the front, up the path, knock on the door and ask, 'Can I have me ball back, mister?' because we didn't want the residents getting all hot and bothered about us and having us banned from using the field.

But it's a long way round and sometimes it's easier just to hop over a fence, grab the ball and hop back. Which was what I was going to do. I could see the ball – but then I saw the dog. I don't know what kind it was but it didn't look like the sort of dog you'd pat on the head. Not if you wanted to keep your fingers. Or your hand.

This dog didn't bound about barking like some of them do. At least you know where you are with them. This one was just lying there with one eye open and its tongue lolling out. I could just make out the teeth glistening. Was it tied up? Was it friendly? Was it hungry?

I started to put one leg over the fence. Bam! I didn't know dogs could move so fast from a standing start – or rather, a lying start. Just one bark – '*Raaaaarf!*' – and a fur-covered missile with teeth at the sharp end flew across the garden. I brought my leg back smartish and Fido slammed into the wooden railing with a bang. I hardly had time to get my balance when the head appeared over the top of the fence and snarled at me as if I was the worst thing it had ever come across. It was as if I'd kidnapped its owner, or tried to feed it vegeburgers. And it didn't even know me!

The rest of the lads were falling over laughing. It made the loss of the ball almost worthwhile to them. Of course, I trotted round the front, all set to go and knock and ask politely, but Old Friendly Fido was waiting for me at the front gate – so I didn't risk it.

We had a spare ball, so we left the other one for Fido to look after. I said I'd go round later and try and get it back. I wasn't popular but, as I said, being the joke of the evening almost made it worth it.

I did go back later, but I wished I hadn't. Fido was still there and the house was in darkness. I waited at the gate for a minute or two but no one came to see what the barking was about. Except, just as I was about to leave, a voice said, '*Eelavya-eewill!*'

I jumped. What? I looked round – and I jumped

again. There was an enormous creature looking down at me. The sound came again and there was a sort of grim pleasure in the way it spoke.

'You wanna be careful. Eelavya!'

I realized that the first thing it had said was: 'He'll have you, he will.' I had no doubt that the voice was right. I thought I should say something.

'Um, I was trying to get my ball back. We were playing over the back – in the playing field . . .'

'My lass's kids like football,' said the voice, and I realized that the creature was female – and was someone's granny. I'm glad she wasn't mine – though she would have been useful in a scrap. She was huge. Her arms reached down to her knees like she'd been carrying shopping bags full of lead for fifty years, and her face looked as if it had driven a tunnel through the Alps and left the mountains feeling shaky.

'Oh yes,' she went on. 'Great ones for the football. You wanna come and meet them?'

'Um, not now,' I stammered. 'I've got to get home. Just called by on my way to see if I could get the ball . . .'

'You won't see that again,' she said. 'Not if I know Winnie.'

'Winnie?'

'That's his name. Short for something else, I think.' The human hill turned away and carried on up the street.

So I didn't get the ball back. As if that wasn't bad enough, two days later I did the same thing! Well, not exactly the same thing, but near enough. I booted the ball and it shot into a garden three doors down from the dog-lover's one. This time I didn't try getting over the back. Anyway, there was a hawthorn hedge and it would have hurt. I went round the front, up the path and rang the bell. It was the sort of bell you can't hear so you don't know if it works or not. So you bang on the door knocker and then someone comes and says, 'All right, all right, give us a chance, first the bell, now the knocker . . .'

But it didn't get to that stage. A woman answered the door straight away. I hadn't met her before but there was something oddly familiar about her face.

'Hello?' she said. 'I don't want to buy anything.'

'I'm not selling anything,' I replied. 'I just came to get our ball back.'

'Oh,' she said. 'Come in.'

Come in? The ball would be in the garden. Why would I want to go in? But I did. I didn't want to upset her and risk not getting the ball back. My position in the team might be at risk if I lost another one.

I followed her into the front room. There were three little kids in there. The telly was on and there on the telly was the football! Great! I thought. This is easier than I expected.

One of the kids, a lad of about five, looked up. 'I'm Simon,' he said. 'I play football.'

'Oh,' I said. 'Good. So do I.'

'Simon found the ball,' said his mum. 'He's very keen on football. That's why he wanted to meet you.'

'I like football too!' shouted another of the kids. This one looked a bit older and had hair sticking straight up like he'd stuck a finger in the electric socket. In case we hadn't heard, he said, even louder, '*I like football too!*'

'Good,' I said. 'So do I.'

The third kid was a girl. She was staring at the telly.

She didn't look up but she spoke very clearly. 'I'm better than both of them.'

'Oh,' I said. 'Good.'

I didn't want to have a longer conversation. I just wanted the ball.

'Could I have the ball, please?'

'Get the young man his ball,' said the mum. She nodded towards the television. The ball was sitting in an ashtray, which stopped it rolling off. Next to it was a big photo of the three kids. They were with some kind of monster. I looked again . . . Yikes! It was the Gruesome Gran I had met the other day. That's why her daughter looked familiar, poor woman.

They must have seen me staring because the mum said, 'That's their gran. She likes football too. Grandad used to play for Barton First Team.'

Wow, I thought. Granny made Mountain Boy look average. Never mind Grandad, maybe *she'd* like to play for us. I looked again at the expression on her face and thought, perhaps not. I've got enough trouble with Big Foot.

Electric Hair got up and took the ball off the telly. I didn't like the way he held on to it so tightly as he spoke.

'You good at football?'

'Not bad.'

'You play in a team?'

'Yeah. Barrow Boys. On the wing. On the right. Can't kick with me left. Not many people can.'

'You gonna give us some training?'

'Eh?' What was he on about? Me – training?

'Some practice. That's what we want. You play for a team. You can do it.'

I looked at the mother, hoping that she would

intervene. All she needed to say was, 'Come along. Just give the young man his ball back, so he can get back to his friends. They must be wondering where he is . . .' I could imagine the words perfectly. Any adult could manage them. But she didn't.

Instead, she said, 'What a good idea! I'm sure he'd give you some help in return for you getting the ball for him.' She looked at me. What could I say? I wanted the ball. I could hardly say, 'Look, I'm not that good myself and if you think I'm going to be seen out with this lot teaching them football skills, you must be madder than the dog three doors down.'

Bitter experience had taught me that honesty wasn't always appreciated, especially in a young person.

The girl spoke again, still not taking her eyes off the television. 'Tomorrow, then, four o'clock.'

'Yeah,' said Simon. 'That'll be great.'

Electric Hair just looked at me. I nodded. 'Sure,' I said. 'Why not?' I stared at the ball. He gave it to me. 'It's a deal,' he said. I scooted out of that house and ran back to the playing field.

'Where have you been?' shouted Big Foot. 'Having tea?'

I booted the ball to him and yelled, 'You can go next time!'

'Only if I'm stupid enough to kick it over,' he replied and sped off down the pitch.

The match against Barton was on Saturday and we only had two days to improve. Another problem was that Mountain Boy was away visiting his dad some-where. This was going to be a tough game.

Once or twice I remembered the promise I'd made, but I pushed it out of my mind. Some other time, maybe. Anyway, I'd been *forced* to make the deal; it wasn't fair. I needed all the practice I could get myself if I wanted to secure my place in the team. I couldn't afford to be belting the ball into any more back yards, that was for sure.

We had a bit of trouble finding the ball for the match but we found it in the end. It was the same one that I'd booted over the hedge earlier in the week.

'This time, if I pass to you, pass it back!' rasped Gonzo.

Not much point in passing it in the first place, I thought – but I didn't say it. I nodded. We trooped onto the field and the match began.

It was tough. The Barton lads were bigger than we were – and fitter. But we were on our home ground and we didn't like to be beaten there. I was playing all right until, about halfway through the first half, I noticed them on the touchline. It was the three kids – Simon, Electric Hair and The Girl.

I thought they'd come to support us until I heard them shouting at me.

'Useless!' called out Electric Hair as I passed the ball to the opposition. The Girl shouted something ruder. I realized that they hadn't forgotten my broken promise.

It's funny how something like that can put you off your game. I just couldn't get a pass right and every time I got the ball and set off down the wing, they'd start yelling and I'd let it go over the line or the Barton winger would just stroll up and take it off me.

When the half-time whistle went, we were two–nil down and I was ready to quit.

Big Foot just looked at me – but he didn't say anything, and I was grateful for that. I thought he might ask who my friends on the touchline were.

We got ready to kick off for the second half. I looked over to the touchline. They weren't there. Of course, they'd change sides so they could be closer to me so I could hear their insults better.

No, they weren't there either. Yippee! They'd got tired and given up. I was going to give it everything for the next forty-five minutes.

Things went better for a while but we couldn't pull back those two goals. There were twenty minutes to go when I spotted the Loathsome Three again. They were walking in a line towards the pitch. But they weren't alone. Leading them was a woman, a very large woman.

'Yikes! It's Gruesome Gran!' I blurted out. What was she doing here? Had she come to add her voice to their insults and catcalls?

It was worse than that.

The four of them approached like soldiers marching to a funeral, but a funeral they were going to enjoy. Big Gran strode straight onto the pitch. There were a few cries of 'Oi!' and 'Hey?' but then play faltered and stopped. They all looked up at her, wondering, as I had done when I first met her, what kind of creature this was. The ball dribbled to a halt. Near me, as it happened.

Gruesome Gran and the Nightmare Kids walked straight to the ball. The players gaped at her. She looked at them, she looked at me and then she looked down at the ball. Slowly and deliberately she bent down and picked up the ball. She turned to me again. I didn't dare look up. I might turn to stone.

Her voice rasped out. 'You promised them and you let them down. That's not good enough, Mister Young Footballer. No practice. No ball. No deal.'

No one questioned her. With that she stalked off the pitch, ball in hand, and the three kids behind her like ducklings behind a very large mother duck. Electric Hair turned round and stuck his tongue out at me, but the other two ignored me.

The match had to be abandoned. There was no other ball. I slunk off to get changed, expecting my days in the Barrow Boys team to be at an end. How was I going to explain my way out of this one? Buttertoes was nothing. What would the captain call me now?

I was surprised when Big Foot grinned at me. 'Don't worry,' he said. 'It was an old ball. And anyway, we were going to lose the game. By the time we have a rematch, Mountain Boy will be back. It couldn't have happened at a better time. See you on Tuesday for a practice!'

'Yeah,' I said, 'Sure.' But playing at home has never been the same since. I keep checking the touchline for the three kids. I keep scanning the horizon for the huge bulk of Gruesome Gran. I've stopped kicking the ball into back gardens, though. And I'm very careful about what promises I make.

Striking Out

Pat Leighton

Chris Davenport, mid-centre for Blexford Town's
Under-13s football team, sat on the changing room
bench getting kitted up for the mid-week practice. He
was in a mess, a stinking, awful, sick-making mess –
and he was going to do something about it.

He'd told himself that his brother, Matt, was the
whole trouble. But how could you blame someone
who was dead? Someone you could only just
remember? You could if your mum never let you forget
him:

Just like your big brother you are, football in the
blood – an absolute natural, he was ... The Albion
cubs was only the beginning, everybody said so ... A
top professional in the making, you ask your Uncle
Eddie and Uncle Pete ...

His uncles. His mother's brothers. They'd been
around for ever, both ex-professionals, both feeding
him stories of football the way other uncles told
bedtime stories. It had been OK when he was younger.
There was always a football on the lawn, new gear
from Uncle Eddie's sports shop.

His dad used to give him a kick-around but it was
the uncles who really pushed him on, got him into the
'little' leagues, yelled him on in all the school matches.

His dad just grinned and cheered in the right places and said 'well done' whether they'd lost or won.

And he'd loved it then: all the excitement, the mud, the frantic running, the over-the-top celebration scrums of little lads when they scored a goal. He'd learnt a lot since the early days, of course, but that word was always cropping up.

'You've got a *natural* there, Helen,' his uncles would say to his mum.

He was a 'natural' midfielder, a 'natural' right-footer, a 'natural' for finding space. When he'd been small he'd thought that 'being a natural' meant you were very good at football. Well, that was OK. He *was* a good footballer.

He was older now, though, and beginning to think for himself. He was good because he'd put hours into it. Ever since he could remember, football had filled every minute of his spare time. What had changed over this last season? He supposed it was palling up with Alec. That, and the arrival of Jason Gilmore.

He was jerked back to the here and now as Timmo, one of his best mates, came crashing in late and threw his ancient hold-all down onto the bench.

'Hey up, Davvy! Shift over and give us a bit of room,' Timmo cried, cheerful as ever.

Chris shuffled up. There was no waiting with Timmo – you moved or got sat on. But Chris wasn't in the mood for yakking and jokes. He muttered a brief 'hi' and put his head down, pretending to concentrate on his boot laces.

Not that Timmo noticed. Arms everywhere, he was busy rooting around for his goalkeeping gear.

'Come on, let's get out there and murder some turf!'

Timmo said, and he was off for the door, still half-dressing himself.

Chris gave his laces a last tug. He watched Timmo go and wondered what he'd say if he knew that Chris was thinking of throwing the District Cup Final. He didn't even dare think what the rest of his team-mates would say. Just thinking about it set his nerves on edge. He slipped past a few stragglers in the hut, swung himself down the wooden steps and ran onto the town's recreation pitch.

Just under two weeks to the final and everybody was warming up with a vengeance. Chris picked up a loose practice ball on his toe and went off on a circuit: dribble-trap, dribble-trap. He didn't much mind where so long as he had his own space, and time to think some more.

How *did* you throw a match, anyway? He'd read about it in the newspapers, heard reports on television . . . but how did you actually go about it? It wasn't something he'd ever thought about before, but he couldn't see any other way. He paused in a quiet corner of the pitch and kept his feet busy with a sequence of ball-control skills he could do in his sleep now. His mind was still racing. He supposed he didn't really mean *throw* the match. He didn't want the team to lose – they'd never got this far in the cup before – he just wanted to play a bad match himself.

Who was he kidding! It would take every ounce of talent the team had to come up with a winner against Delingham Youths. This year was the first they had ever been strong enough to touch Delingham, in the league or cup, and Delingham were still strong favourites. If he played below par it would make a difference, no two ways about it.

Just then the whistle blew and Todd Mackenzie, the coach, yelled across the pitch, 'Come on, you lot! Let's get this session under way.'

Chris took an angry stab at the ball and chased after it. It wasn't fair. And it wasn't Matt's fault, either. It was his mum's and those uncles of his. Why hadn't he got the guts to stand up to them? To tell them what he'd decided? How he was really feeling?

He swung into the exercises Mac was pacing them through, and on to the skills. At least it took his mind off what he was planning. He wove between skittles, played right foot, left, dodged, passed, flicked. He was good at it, he knew he was; rock solid. If he played at his very best, he was good enough to catch the eye of the Albion scouts. The First Division club in the city was always on the lookout for promising cubs. Everyone knew they'd be at the final.

But he didn't want it. Not any more.

He drew up behind a line of his sweaty team-mates waiting to practise shooting. He took a few deep breaths, hands on hips. Jason Gilmore was just about to make his run. Chris watched. So did most of the rest of them. Jason was probably the main reason they were in the final. He'd joined the club just after Christmas. He'd moved down from up north and had been a striker in the county team up there. Mac had no doubt he could go a long way in the game.

Jason was perfection; cool as an iceberg and spot on with every move. He flowed towards the goal, flicked with an outside foot. Poor old Timmo didn't even have a chance of guessing which way the ball would go.

'Pity you can't change your name to Matt,' Chris thought ruefully to himself, as he watched the blond striker move effortlessly away with the ball centimetres from his feet.

The very first time he'd seen Jason in action, it had hit him. That was what a natural was; that was what his brother Matt must have been before the lorry had jack-knifed on a wet road and wiped him off the crossing.

He'd never be a Jason or a Matt. That was what he'd faced up to. He had plenty of skills, he could even go further than the Town Boys, but he would never be the 'star' his mother had in her head; the dreams his uncles had in theirs.

The coach blew the whistle for a half-hour game to finish off. If Chris was serious about it, now was the time to give it a try.

For the first time in his life, Chris didn't give it one hundred per cent. He started in for tackles a second or two later than he would have done normally. He eased up slightly in mid-run, then made it look good by spurting – too late – at the end. He even managed two shots which just skimmed the side bars.

'What's up, Davvy?' Timmo shouted, his grin showing that he was joking. 'Giving me a rest before the big match?'

'Nah, just getting you to stretch your lazy muscles,' Chris joked back.

All the same, the next time he had the ball near the box he sent a carefully aimed pass straight to Jason, who slammed it past Timmo.

'Thanks a lot!' Timmo snorted at the pair of them.

Chris slapped Jason on the back and they jogged back upfield. He really did work well with the new striker, liked him in fact, even if he was a bit stand-offish. But mainly he didn't want to overdo the mediocre stuff.

For the rest of the practice, Chris played his usual sound game. He even enjoyed it, felt the thrill in his boots, the head-rush of a good run downfield.

Back in the changing hut, as they all clambered and struggled for their gear, he knew one thing for certain. If he wanted to, he could play a duff game without making it too obvious.

Mac's voice rising above the mayhem broke in on his thoughts. Everyone in the hut went quiet. When Mac spoke, you listened.

'Right,' said Mac, 'no match this weekend so I'll expect to see you all out for practice on Saturday and Sunday. Gym session as usual on Tuesday, and we'll have a final practice before the big one next Thursday. Any questions? No? OK, get lost and don't break a leg!'

Outside, Chris strapped his bag onto his bike and slowly made his way home.

'Tea's in the oven,' his mother said as soon as he walked through the door.

It would be, he thought.

He sat himself down, elbows on the table, chin in his hands. Might as well enjoy the peace before the usual interrogation started. Straight ahead of him on the sideboard was Matt's photo, the one that had always been there, the one of him in his Albion strip. Chris knew it was mean of him to blame Mum. If *he* was dead, he'd want her to remember him.

It was just that the two of them looked so much alike: same haywire brown hair, same eyes, same build even. Sometimes, just sometimes, he wasn't sure whether his mum was talking about Matt or him.

'Here you are,' said his mum, placing a steaming bowl of chicken casserole in front of him. 'Food for the troops. How did the practice go?'

'Fine,' Chris replied, tearing apart a bread roll and stuffing some in his mouth. Couldn't talk with his mouth full, could he?

'Do well, did you?'

He spooned in some casserole and nodded. Not that she waited for an answer anyway.

'Great. Tell Mr Mackenzie not to forget to let me have the strips for the final well in time. Have to make a special effort with them, won't I!'

That was another thing. She didn't only turn up at all the matches. She washed the match strips, helped with refreshments – there was no escape. He was just thankful she didn't trot on as team mascot as well! Luckily, his dad came in with his tea at that point and started talking to him about some wildlife film or other he'd seen.

Give me wildlife over Mum any day of the week, Chris thought to himself.

His luck didn't last, though. The back door opened and his two uncles breezed into the kitchen.

'Getting psyched up for the big match then, Chris? Not long to go now,' said his Uncle Eddie, giving him a thump between the shoulder blades.

'Of course he is! One of us, isn't he? Thinks positive,' his Uncle Pete laughed. 'Just turn it on for those scouts, mate. Got an old contact of mine from United coming over to have a look, too. Do your best and you'll be in, no sweat.'

'He always does his best, just like Matt always did,'

187

his mother chimed up, 'and he'll get just as far, you mark my words.'

Chris couldn't stand it any more. He pushed his chair away from the table and made for the door.

'Where are you going?' his mum asked, surprised.

'Over to Alec's. Said I'd help him with his bike. Be about an hour.'

Out in the hallway he grabbed his anorak. As he tugged at the zip, he heard his dad's voice.

'Why don't you lot leave the poor lad alone?' he said mildly.

'Oh, *y-o-o-u* . . .' he heard his mum reply, in that voice she always used when she thought his dad was probably right but she wasn't going to admit it.

At least he could get everything off his chest down at Alec's. *He* wasn't football mad – and he listened. The two of them had been going round with each other for most of this school year, ever since they'd landed up in the same class.

Alec was into bikes; properly into them, belonged to a racing club and everything. Chris had never liked mountain bikes much; he had a pretty good road bike himself. Alec had helped him sort out some upgrades that he was going to ask for next birthday. He'd even been out on a couple of rides with the club and had a great time. They'd said he could go any time, and he would, too, when the football season was over. Same old story!

Once he had started helping to clean up Alec's stripped-down bike and had told him everything, Chris cooled down. Alec did his best to help.

'How do you know you'll make the grade with the scouts anyway? Sounds as if this Jason would be the first choice.'

'You can't make a team out of eleven strikers, or geniuses like Jason Gilmore. They'll be looking for good all-rounders, too,' said Chris.

That was him to a T.

'I just don't want it, Alec,' he said. 'Do you know how many cubs actually make it to senior level?'

Alec grunted between the screw he had clasped in his teeth and shook his head.

'Not many, I can tell you,' Chris went on. 'Imagine it, all those months – years even – the hours of playing before they tell you, *Sorry, lad, but* . . .'

Something else was niggling him, something he didn't even want to tell Alec. How many ears had 'the uncles' bent about him? Were they trying to pull strings? He hoped not, but it was one more reason to stick to his plan now that he had made up his mind.

'I don't reckon you can do it,' Alec said.

'What do you mean?'

'It's OK in a practice,' said Alec, 'but can you really see yourself backing off in the actual match, not wanting to win, letting your mates down?'

'I won't be letting them down! I'm not the whole ruddy team, you know!'

'Why not just take a sicky, then? Come up with some mysterious bug? Or play your usual game and say "no thank you" when the scouts recognize your outstanding talents?' Alec said, half-jokingly.

Chris shot him a sarcastic look. 'You have *met* my mum – and the uncles?'

Alec pulled a face. 'More than once. It was just a thought. Best of luck, that's all I can say. Want me to come along and watch?'

'So you can pick up the pieces? No thanks.'

*

189

It was here. The day of the final. The inside of the Town Boys' changing room buzzed as if it was wired with high-voltage electricity. Chris looked around. Jack Briggs, who ran midfield with him, gave him his 'I am an alien' impression as he pushed his head through his crisp, royal-blue match shirt. Timmo was high as a kite and already plucking imaginary balls out the air. Jason was as cool as ever, a quiet smile on his face but his eyes sparkling, ready for anything. Real winner's eyes.

The door opened. A smell of outside and the hum of voices came in with Mac, and went as he shut the door behind him. They weren't at any of their usual venues. It was a tradition for the county non-pro club to offer their ground for the District Final, so it was like the real thing: terraces, a small stand, loudspeakers, the lot, even the county ref and linesmen.

'OK,' said Mac, 'this is it. You know you can do it, so just go out there and give it all you've got. *And enjoy it!*'

They all groaned at the old clichés.

'I mean it,' said Mac. 'Now come on, let's show Delingham what for.'

They clattered out after him. Chris hung back and walked out with Timmo.

'How are you feeling, Chris?' his friend asked, tossing a ball from hand to hand.

'Nervous!' Well, that was true enough.

'Me too,' said Timmo, his grin coming back. He rolled his eyes heavenwards. 'Please, God, help me to keep 'em out.' And he was off down the field, heading for a pair of goalposts.

Chris sprinted into midfield and began a kick-around with Jack. Whistle, toss, ends, positions; he went through the familiar routine as if he was only half there. He looked round. The ground wasn't exactly crowded out, but it might as well have been for all the noise the families and friends of the two sides were making.

He could see his lot, too, behind the barriers, bang on the centre line. His mum waved. His Uncle Pete nodded towards a row of stand seats, pointed with his raised arm. The scouts, Chris supposed. His uncle gave him the thumbs-up sign. The ref raised the whistle to his mouth and blew. The game was on.

Everything was fine for the first ten minutes. The Delingham players were as nervous as the Town Boys and Chris got by, playing a steady but unspectacular game – nothing to bring him to any scout's attention, one way or the other. Then a Delingham winger broke.

Now, thought Chris. He left his run a fraction late and his leading foot met fresh air as the winger sailed past him. Trouble was, he sailed past Liam, one of their backs, too, and sent a corker screaming across to the big Delingham striker everybody knew all too well. Wham! Timmo caught it, safe as houses. Chris breathed a sigh of relief and ran back upfield. He told himself Timmo would be glad to have got into the game, to have the ball between his gloves. He tried not to think how he'd have felt if Timmo had missed – and Delingham had scored.

They did, five minutes later, but the play was well away from Chris. There was nothing he could have done about it.

After that, Delingham piled on the pressure but the Town Boys fought back. Chris could feel his team-mates' determination so strongly he could almost touch it. Liam blocked another Delingham charge and smartly sent the ball up to Chris. It was an obvious chance for a quick break but Chris held back, dribbled right a bit, left a bit.

'Chris!' screamed Jack. He moved in, took the ball and flicked it forward to Jason. Jason was off across the pitch, slicing through the defence like butter. He turned and sent such a good ball across the goal mouth that all Wilkie, their other striker, had to do was stick out his foot. One–all. The crowd erupted and the ecstatic Town forwards raced back to the centre, grabbing every blue shirt they could on the way back. Jack didn't join in. He was on his way over to Chris.

'Thumping heck, Chris, what was all that about?' he asked, half puzzled, half angry.

Chris could feel himself going red. 'Nothing, sorry,' he mumbled and ran back to position, waiting for the whistle. His head was in a whirl. The look on Jack's face! Then he gritted his teeth. He hadn't done anything drastic, put them in any real trouble. He couldn't give in now.

He didn't, but the rest of the half was like hell. No way was he going to mess up something vital, but whenever he thought the team was in a pretty safe position he stuck to his plan: a corner even Gascoigne couldn't have converted, a few kicks into touch, tackles that stopped short of being real tackles.

Then, just before the half-time whistle, the Town made a break. The ball was with Chris and Jason was right where he knew he'd be, running into a space on the right ready to take it. So was the green shirt of a Delingham centre-back. He sent the ball just slightly towards the Delingham player, his heart pounding with more than the effort of the game. If Jason was really quick he'd get it anyway, he thought. He didn't. The green shirt got there first and the Delingham player charged up the pitch. The whistle went.

Before he could get anywhere near the half-time team talk, Chris's arm was clenched in a tight grip and Jason swung him round to face him.

'I don't know what you're playing at, Davenport,' he spat out, narrowing his eyes, 'but a few more dumb moves like that and you'll have lost us the match. Pull yourself together.'

He didn't even wait for a reply. Chris swallowed hard. He felt rotten. He felt even worse when he joined the rest of the team and saw the down-beaten looks on their faces.

'Come on, you lot! It's one–all, not ten–nil. You're doing great!' Mac enthused. And by the time he'd finished ten more minutes of the same build-up they were all looking a lot happier. 'That's more like it,' he said. 'Now get out there and finish them off.'

But as they broke up, he caught Chris by the arm.

'Don't let it get to you, Chris,' he said quietly. 'Just play your normal game. We'd never have got this far without you in midfield. Remember that.'

Chris went back onto the pitch with his mind in turmoil. He hadn't been as clever as he thought. Mac had noticed – except Mac thought he was letting the big match get to him. He could see the others, high on adrenalin, raring to go. Would they think that, too? That he'd bottled out? Then he saw Jack and Jason talking, heads together, and looking over at him. Timmo joined them. Chris could see him waving his arms about, shaking his head. No guesses what they were saying. What should he do?

With the first touch of the ball, clear as a bell, he knew. It was nothing to do with Matt, his mum or anyone else; it was his decision. He'd do what Mac said, play his normal solid game. He'd probably done enough to put the scouts off in the first half, anyway!

He made mistakes. It wasn't that easy, switching his head round from playing for himself to being part of the team, and at first he had a sneaking feeling that Jack wasn't sending all the passes he usually would. But gradually he got back into the swing of things and his game began to flow. With the team in this mood, he could hardly help it anyway. He'd never seen them like this – playing with everything they'd got and then some. And he was in on it, one of them again. It felt brilliant. Alec was right, he'd been an idiot. Now he'd do his best to make up for it.

But Delingham weren't favourites for nothing. They were pushing like mad and it was taking every ounce of effort and determination for the Town Boys to hold them. Twice Jason broke through, twice a horde of green shirts blocked him. There was not much time left and both teams knew it. Chris had the ball, Jack was with him. They took it upfield between them. Jason feinted, left his marker and ran across in front for a forward pass. The mid-centres ran on as he flew like a rocket down the wing and swept in towards goal. The keeper came out, Jason flicked back. It was on Chris's right foot before he knew it – the perfect ball, an open goal.

He hesitated for a split second, something he would never have done normally. This was his chance to put things right, he mustn't make a mistake. Even as he thought it, he felt the charge and his feet went from under him as a burly Delingham back smashed the ball off his boot. A sickening wrench went through his ankle and a fierce pain shot up his leg as he hit the turf.

Mac took no chances. Chris was on the bench and stringy Darryl Wright, their sub, was haring off across the pitch as if he couldn't believe his luck. Chris didn't know whether to laugh or cry. How about that for showing the scouts what he could do? It was almost as if he'd asked for it! He buried his head in his hands, wincing as Mac propped up his foot.

Then he heard a roar and Mac was on his feet, jumping around like a demented kangaroo. Chris looked up in time to see Darryl go sprawling in the box. Somehow he'd got his foot to the ball and sent it skying towards Jason. The tall striker rose, his head met it like a dream and he cracked it into the top left-hand corner of the net. The crowd erupted, Mac was yelling and pumping the air with both fists, blue shirts swamped the Delingham area and went mad. They were ahead! All they had to do now was hold on.

Chris forgot everything else for those last few minutes. He went as wild as the rest of them when the final whistle blew and he knew that the team had won. There was pandemonium – they even had him on his good foot and dancing around until Mac rescued him. He saw the scouts coming over to congratulate Mac, saw one of them strolling over in Jason's direction.

Suddenly his dad was there. Behind him Chris could see the rest of the family and the excitement drained out of him.

'Well done, lad,' said his dad. 'Great match, you lot. Thanks for everything, Mac. I'll get that foot to the hospital for a check-up, just to make sure. You go back home in Eddie's car, Helen. I'll give you a ring from casualty.' There was no mistaking the firmness in his voice. He helped Chris over to the car park and had him in the car before his mum had even moved.

'Thanks, Dad,' Chris said weakly. The pain was getting to him now and he felt a bit sick.

'Don't mention it, son,' said his dad, giving Chris a big wink as he opened the passenger window to let in some fresh air.

Chris took in a few deep breaths and closed his eyes. He finally had it sorted. He wouldn't stop playing with Town Boys – he enjoyed it too much – but that was as far as it was going. He'd give the cycling a proper go, do some real training, and if that meant missing the odd football practice, so what? It wasn't the end of the world. There was still his mum and the uncles to handle but he'd manage it somehow. What he needed was to get somebody onside with him. He glanced across at his dad and grinned. He'd do! He couldn't think why he hadn't thought of it before. He'd have a good talk with him later.

He relaxed into the seat and let the wind fan his face. 'Move over, life. Make way for Christopher Davenport,' he said silently.

He was on his way.

He's the Man!

David Clayton

One Saturday morning in March, the entire St Mary's
Juniors football team were feeling fed up. Most people
who have just won six–nil are happy – but they
weren't.

After the game they went to the burger bar as usual.
They were saying goodbye to Mighty Mark Mullen.
Soon he would be far away in America and they would
have no goalkeeper.

'You'll be OK. You've got the Professor!' Mark said
and they groaned.

The Professor, Paul Parker, was tall enough and keen
enough. Nobody knew more than him about the game.
He had everything – except talent. If he put his head
in his hands, he'd drop it!

The lads couldn't bear to talk about it. They knew
that putting the Prof in goal would never work, but
they didn't want to make Mark feel bad.

'Do you *have* to go?' Tom Smith, the captain, wasn't
a softie but even he had a lump in his throat. Mark
was brilliant. If he wasn't diving at people's feet, he
was catching high crosses. If he wasn't catching high
crosses, he was hurling the ball to the half-way. With
him, St Mary's were great; without him they were
ordinary.

Once, Mark had been away on holiday and the

Professor couldn't play either. Steven 'Stick-'em-up' Stanley had been brought in and it had been a disaster.

They called him 'Stick-'em-up' because he held his hands wide apart above his head like the victim of a robbery. Anything right over his head was in. They drew five–all against a terrible team. It was a sad memory. Now they'd have the same problem every game.

Monday came and Miss Murray met the team.

'It's St Joseph's on Saturday. What shall we do about a keeper?' she asked.

There was no reply.

'Ann Bowers is very good,' she said. 'She can catch anything.'

The striker, Adam Roberts pulled a face. 'That's true, miss, but she's got a netball tournament.'

'What about Paul?'

'No. Drops it too often.'

'Steven Stanley?'

'No way!' they roared.

Miss Murray's face went pink.

'Well then, lads,' she said. 'If none of my ideas are any good, *you* sort it out.'

And she turned and walked off.

Chalky looked at Tubby. Adam looked at Butch. Charlie looked at Des.

Finally, Tom said, 'You know something. It *might* have to be the Prof or nobody!'

The team were *not* happy.

It was a miserable day. The game in the yard was duller than usual. Tom sighed as he went over to talk to the Prof. Suddenly there was a shout. Tom turned to see the ball hurtling towards him. There was no time to move.

Whap! A great long arm with a big hand on the end of it appeared in front of Tom's face. He turned and looked up at the body that went with it. The towering boy held the ball *in one hand!*

'Hey!' said the boy in an American accent. 'A guy could get hurt round here!'

The giant beamed down at Tom and shook his dreadlocked head. Then he gave the ball a little flick and spun it on one finger without even looking at it.

'Wow!' gasped Tom. 'Who are *you?*'

'Harrison T. Eccles,' said the lad. 'I'm in England for a year. Mark Mullen's dad and my dad exchanged jobs.'

Now he let the ball roll down his arm on to his neck. He ducked forward and it rolled on down his back and into his other hand behind him.

'Dead easy!' said Stick-'em-up Stanley, looking green with envy.

'OK, man, be my guest!' Harrison flicked the ball to Stanley who dropped it on the floor. Everyone burst out laughing.

'Give him a dustbin. Then he'll be able to catch it!' someone shouted.

Steven Stanley booted the ball away and stomped into school, looking furious. How could he compete with *that?*

Meanwhile the mob had closed round the new boy.

'Hey, how would you like to play football for our team?' asked Adam.

'Soccer? I don't know anything about that!' said Harrison. 'It looked pretty rough out there when you were playing.'

He looked at the scuffed knees of their trousers. Tom had blood coming through his where Adam had tripped him up. Tom hadn't noticed and didn't feel it in the heat of battle.

'No, you'll be OK,' said Tom. 'We just need someone who could teach you.'

Just then the Prof came strolling by playing a computer game.

'And I know just the right person to do it. Paul! Paul! Come here!'

Tom explained the situation to the Prof. The lads watched Tom waving his arms and the Prof shaking his head.

'You have *got* to be joking! By *Saturday*?' The Prof was horrified.

'We need him, really need him, otherwise . . .' Tom stopped – even he could see what he had been going to say. He never did think much.

'Otherwise you're stuck with me or Stanley?' the Prof said sadly.

'Hmm . . . er . . . well . . .' Tom was turning pink.

'OK,' agreed the Prof. 'But it won't be easy.'

'You're brilliant!' muttered Tom. 'I know you can do it!'

Just then the ball came flying across the yard towards Harrison. This time it was ankle high. The big boy craned over but missed it. It was less than a metre from his feet. Harrison was good in the air, but low balls seemed to be a problem!

Why did I agree? thought the Prof. 'I'll get a roasting if we lose now!'

Harrison and the Prof were strolling in the yard together.

'Haven't you *ever* played soccer, not even once?'

'Well, the Hispanic guys played all that stuff. Me, being black *and* a beanpole, I played basketball.'

'You mean, "No, I haven't played".'

'No.'

Down at the other end of the yard, Tom and his mates were all laughing and joking. They thought they'd solved their problem. It was a good job they didn't know what the Prof was thinking.

'Do you know the rules?' the Prof asked, but not hopefully.

'Sort of.'

'Do you know what a goalkeeper is?'

Harrison grinned.

'Yep, got that one. He's like a goalminder in ice hockey, isn't he?'

'Let's go out on the field.'

It was easier to *show* him. Steve Stanley tagged along.

'Man, this is messy!' Harrison looked out on the sea of mud, then down at his trendy trainers. 'No way! These cost me a hundred and fifty dollars!' He perched on a little bank behind the goal. 'Now *this* is OK,' he said.

'He can't keep goal from five metres behind the nets!' Steve chipped in.

'I know! I *know!*' snarled the Prof. It wasn't like him to be ratty but the whole thing was getting to him.

'Stay there!' he snapped. 'We'll show you what you can do if you're a keeper.'

The Prof trudged out on to the swamp. Steve Stanley stood with Harrison.

The Prof pointed downfield. 'Goalkeepers can handle the ball in this area.'

'Wow! That's kinda small. I mean, can't be more than six paces out.'

The Prof could feel his head caving in.

'Not *that* area,' he explained, pointing to the six-yard box. 'The area out to *that* line!' And off he went, stomping round the line like an angry gnome.

'OK, man, but you just didn't say. You said . . .'

'I know! I know!' groaned the Prof.

'But you didn't say, did you?' Steve added.

Ten minutes later, the Prof was walking gloomily back towards the school. It was going to be a hard week.

'Well, I guess I know about goalminding now,' smiled Harrison. 'How about me teaching you basketball?'

The Prof sighed. Saturday stood like a dark cloud before him.

The next day, the Prof brought a big box to school. At break, he opened it in his form-room. Inside the box was a table football game.

'Great!' said Tom.

'Yeah!' chortled Adam. 'We'll all play.'

'Oh, no, you *won't*!' growled Harrison's coach. 'This is to teach Harrison how to play football.'

Just then Miss Murray came along.

'Out, all you boys!'

'But, miss, I need to teach Harrison to be a goalminder . . . I mean goalkeeper.'

Miss Murray gave the tall American lad a long stare. He looked like a bit of a joker to her.

'OK, but no messing!'

Then they were alone. Harrison watched as the other boy set out the game on the classroom table.

'Hey! This is cool but where are the controls?'

'There *are* no controls. It's not a computer game. We're not going to *play* it. I'm just going to show you where to stand.'

'My feet are kind of big for standing on that diddy little field.'

The Prof turned to see Harrison grinning from ear to ear.

'It isn't funny. The guys in the team will be all over us if we lose.'

Harrison turned to see Tom and his mates with their noses pressed against the window. 'Cool!' he said.

Later, a shivering Harrison was bribed by Tom and the lads to have a game in the yard. The Prof watched from a distance and couldn't believe his eyes. Harrison was saving everything. Then Paul worked it out. Tom had the American on his team. Tom, as captain, always picked the best team so almost everything was blocked before it reached Harrison – *and* the ball was so bouncy that it hardly ever stayed on the ground for long. Harrison's long arms gobbled up all the high, wide shots. He looked like a star, but it was too easy. He needed a stronger opposition if he was to show just how good he was.

After a while, Steve Stanley came up alongside the Prof.

'It won't be like that on Saturday.'

'I know!'

'I was watching you before. You can't show him how to play on a table footy board. He'll have to play a proper game. And someone will have to tell him what to do as he goes along!'

The idea hit the Prof like a flash of lightning. Steven Stanley had said something good for once. In American Football they have a coach shouting orders. That's what he had to do. And make sure that the ball was really light and bouncy so that it wouldn't just dribble along the ground.

Suddenly a shot skidded through Tom's defence and clean through Harrison's giraffe legs. Ice ran through the Prof's heart. Basketball players weren't used to picking up the ball from around their knees!

Tom just laughed and said, 'He was unsighted. That's all. You were in his way.'

Harrison smiled gratefully. The Prof walked away sadly. Steven Stanley came up and muttered, 'He's great with the high balls, but he's rubbish with the low ones! Worse than me!'

The Prof had nothing to say. On Thursday, all years 5 and 6 played football. On Thursday, Harrison would play on a real pitch. It was crunch time for them both. Steven Stanley was smiling.

All day Wednesday, the Prof tried to teach Harrison the basic skills. Harrison was quite clever. He understood the rules when the Prof tested him but it would be a bit different when he was actually out there playing.

When Thursday came, the lads noticed that the American boy had a guitar case with him.

'Are you a rocker, then?' asked Adam.

'No, I play the blues like my dad.'

He took out the guitar and was soon picking out a great rhythm. Just then, Miss Conway came by.

'That's really good. Today's our day for the music teacher. You'll have to play for her.'

'Yes, ma'am.'

The Prof felt his brain frying again. The music tutor came in the afternoon. That was when they were supposed to be playing football.

But he needn't have worried. Just before lunch, rain started to pour down. The field was flooded. There was no chance of playing footy now anyway.

On the Friday, the weather was better and the hall was free. The Prof decided that he would teach Harrison one or two commands.

'When someone runs at you like this, I'll shout *Out!* You come out and block them. I'll also shout *Catch! Punch!* and *Kick!*'

They did a few dummy runs. Harrison was still all arms and legs, but he did get in the way of the ball and he was very quick.

At the end of the session, the American gave the Prof a little dig in the shoulder. 'We'll be OK, bro! You call the shots. I'm the man!'

But the Prof wasn't so sure. All afternoon he watched the others. All afternoon he saw how happy they were, even Steven Stanley who was named as sub after the Prof dropped out, saying he had to help Harrison.

That night the Prof played the match a hundred times in his dreams – or rather, nightmares. All the shots were low, and tall, gangly Harrison was letting in goals by the bucketful. Short-tempered Tom was glaring at the Prof and muttering terrible threats.

Next morning the sky was gloomy, but the bad weather held off. The bumpy St Mary's pitch was in good shape, with just a muddy diamond in the middle of the field.

The changing room was buzzing, especially at the St Joseph's end. All their eyes were on Harrison in his jazzy jersey. From the other end a little ginger tough with a pug nose came over to him.

'You aren't playing, are you?'

'Sure thing, son!' said the giant keeper, giving the kid a little pat on the head. 'Stay tuned!'

The boy slunk back to his team-mates. They were not happy.

Meanwhile the Prof was giving Tom some advice.

'You've got to keep it tight at the back, Tom. You've got to keep them shooting from way out. If you do that he'll catch everything.'

'Yeah, yeah, yeah!' You couldn't teach Tom anything. The teachers at the school had the same problem. 'I know what I'm doing,' he added. 'I wasn't born yesterday!'

Tom always did things his way. At the start of games, he would stay back. He was a good central defender but then Adam would get a goal or two and away Tom would go, glory-hunting down at the other end. Then the other team would break away and there'd be a hole as big as the Channel Tunnel in the middle of their defence.

'Think about it!' shouted the Prof as Tom walked away. Tom got on his nerves sometimes. He never thought anything through properly.

'I'm not thick, you know!' the captain snarled, running outside.

The Prof pumped up the ball like mad.

The ref took it off him. 'It's a bit hard, son!' he said.

'It's muddy out there, sir,' explained the Prof. 'It'll help if the ball's a bit lighter.'

When they kicked off, Tom kept to his word and defended. They had a flat back four. The Prof stood behind the goal, calling the moves for Harrison.

'Go out towards the ball a bit . . . Go left . . . More in line with the ball.'

The Prof's plan was working. It was hard to break through the back four and Tom's tough tackling. When they ran past they were offside. When they shot from way out, Harrison caught the ball easily.

The Prof was happy. Harrison was grinning. However, Tom was *not* happy. The score remained nil–nil. Tom *had* to win. Adam, the flying striker, drifted further and further back. Tom moved up until they met in the middle.

'What're you doing up here? Why aren't you down there?' snapped Adam.

'Because you're down here when you should be up there!' yelled Tom, pointing to where the striker should have been.

Meanwhile, a gap had appeared in the St Mary's defence. The ball was at David James's feet; he was St Joseph's best striker. He was in full stride and Harrison was in big trouble.

'C'mon, you guys, cover me!' he called.

'Out!' roared the Prof and off stormed Harrison.

James saw the fearsome sight coming, took a big swing and almost chopped down the corner flag with his shot.

'You duffer!' yelled one of his team-mates.

He turned in anger.

'All right then! Let him run *you* over!'

'Well played, Harrison!' Steven Stanley shouted from the subs area.

'Didn't do nothin'!' smiled Harrison calmly.

Tom trudged back with a red face to take the goal kick.

'I told you . . .' the Prof started.

Tom turned, giving him the evil eye. 'Don't say anything! I know . . .'

All the rest of the half, Tom was itching to storm upfield again. But every time he thought about it, he could imagine the Prof saying, 'You'll be sorry!'

Then St Mary's won a corner after some tricky footwork by Adam. Their opponents had all eleven back. Tom, Joe, Mark and Jim, all the back four, charged up in spite of the Prof's warnings. The other players were packed like sardines in the other penalty area. Harrison stood alone. There was a huge gap in the middle of the pitch.

'Go out! Go way out!' called the Prof.

'But there's nobody coming and it's kinda muddy out there.' Harrison was happier with dry feet in the sandy goal mouth.

'Just do it, OK?'

Harrison advanced to the penalty spot. 'Here?'

'Further.'

Harrison stopped on the edge of the penalty area. 'Here?'

'Further out,' the Prof pointed.

'But, man, if I go further, I can't handle the ball.' Harrison wasn't happy.

'Further,' nodded the Prof. 'Halfway to the centre.'

Harrison looked round when he got there. 'Hey, this is stupid!'

He stood with his arms folded. He was ankle-deep

in mud like porridge. He was not smiling as he turned towards the Prof.

'Watch the game!' came the cry.

Then the corner came over. It was a bad one. A big defender gave the ball a hefty hoof towards the halfway and the race was on.

'Go get it! Boot it!' yelled the Prof.

Harrison was on his way, teeth gritted, knees flying as if he was riding a bike. He was running one way; twenty others were running the other. *Now* he saw why he was out there.

Whap! He gave the ball an almighty crack. It cleared the St Mary's defence, the St Mary's attack, the ref, the St Joseph's attack and all their defence but one spindly red-haired boy. Just as it was sailing wide, the boy decided to poke his head at it. This was a bad idea. The goalie was in front of him. The ball squiggled, squirmed and spun, slipped and stopped just over the line. Terrible words were spoken. St Mary's jumped for joy.

Harrison T. Eccles smiled.

'I'm the man!' he said.

When half-time came, Harrison was a hero and St Joseph's slunk like ghosts from the field.

'Will you stop jumping out of their goalie's way?' their manager moaned. 'He isn't Arnold Schwarzenegger!'

'But, sir!' protested James. 'He's just so big!'

'He hasn't done anything yet!' snapped the teacher. 'Try to get round the outside. Test him a bit on the ground.'

The second half started. St Mary's were still glowing.

St Joseph's were still steaming. Right away, nippy James switched to wide on the right and sprinted clear.

'Out!' yelled the Prof, and off raced Harrison towards the penalty spot.

'No! No!' screamed the Prof. 'Not out there. Out towards him!'

'You didn't *say*, man!' gasped Harrison as he started to leg it back.

Nearly everyone was laughing. It was obvious now that Harrison had never played before.

James saw his chance and smashed the ball hard and low towards the open goal. Harrison got a leg to it but only succeeded in kneeing the ball violently into the net.

'I don't believe it,' groaned Tom.

As the ball bounced back onto the pitch, Tom lashed out at it. Unfortunately, the ball flew off his boot past the post and smashed the Prof right between the eyes.

'*Aaaaaagh!* I've got mud in my eyes!' he yelled.

'Yeah,' said Harrison, 'and your nose is bleeding.'

The Prof wobbled away towards the school. St Joseph's were looking at Harrison as if he was a turkey at Christmas.

'What do I do now?' said the keeper.

Tom coughed. 'Dunno!' he said.

Sam Carter, St Joseph's captain, was full of glee.

'C'mon. Their keeper's rubbish! We'll hammer them!' he shouted to his team.

And, right away, they were swarming like ants all over St Mary's. Tom went charging at Sam in midfield. The other lad slipped past him and James was on his way towards Harrison again.

This time, he kept his eye on the ball. This time he steadied himself.

210

'Run out at him!' Steven Stanley's voice came from behind the goal. 'Don't dive too soon!'

Again the goalie closed in on the forward. This time the shot was struck hard and low. Suddenly, Harrison's lanky body shot sideways like a spring. A great arm struck like a snake to tip the ball wide. David James was already punching the air to celebrate his goal. Now he stood gaping at the save.

'Great stop!' shouted Steve. 'Now, back post for the corner. Catch it if you can. Punch if you can't.'

Over came a high, looping corner. Harrison punched, but the ball flew almost straight up in the air and fell towards the penalty spot. Sam stood alone to volley it goalwards.

Wham! What a stormer! Fast though it came in, it went out even faster off Harrison's fists, almost taking Sam's head off.

For the rest of the game, Tom held his place and kept the opposition out. On the other hand, Adam was well marked by Sam. One–all was a fair result. At the end, all the players on both teams crowded round to congratulate Harrison.

'Who are you?' was the favourite question from the St Joseph's players.

'I'm Harrison T. Eccles from the USA,' he smiled.

'You're the man!' shouted Steven Stanley as both teams clapped him off the field. Halfway back they met the Prof coming the other way with a bloody hanky over his nose.

'I saw that save. Fantastic!' he said.

'Well, I owe part of it to your good buddy, Steve, here.'

Steve blushed but the Prof grinned as Harrison slapped Steve on the back.

'You're a great coach, Steve!'

'Yes,' said Tom, 'but the Prof's the man for tactics.'

'Hey,' said the giant keeper, 'you know what this means?'

'What?' asked Tom.

'I guess we're all the man!'

And they all laughed.

Terence Blacker
The Transfer

The computer graphic appears on Stanley's screen. A small figure bouncing a tiny white football on his right foot.

His heart thumping, Stanley slips on the headband and places the electrodes against his scalp.

'It works by force of human will,' his mother had said.

The force of Stanley's will is awesome. And he's about to make his wildest, most dangerous dream come true.

Stanley Peterson loves football even more than his computer scientist mother hates it. His obsession takes him on a breathtaking journey into the impossible, where he can become one of the greatest strikers of all time – but where there's a frightening price to pay . . .

'The Transfer is in a league of its own. Blacker fuses two junior obsessions – football and computers – into a compulsively readable story . . . Fantasy football as it should be.' *The Times*

George Layton
The Fib *and other stories*

I was sick of Gordon Barraclough. Sick of his bullying. And I was sick of him being a good footballer. 'Listen, Barraclough. My uncle is Bobby Charlton.'

'You're a liar.'

I was. 'I'm not. Cross my heart and hope to die.' I spat on my left hand. If I'd dropped down dead on the spot I wouldn't have been surprised.

Getting into trouble is much easier than getting out of it in George Layton's bestselling collection of funny, bittersweet stories about growing up in the Fifties.

'A rare gift . . . a book whose appeal extends equally to adults.' *Guardian*

A selected list of titles available from Macmillan and Pan Books

The prices shown below are correct at the time of going to press. However, Macmillan Publishers reserve the right to show new retail prices on covers which may differ from those previously advertised.

GARY LINEKER'S Favourite Football Stories	0 330 35015 3	£4.99
TERENCE BLACKER		
The Transfer	0 330 35173 7	£3.99
Hotshots		
1. Pride and Penalties	0 330 32912 X	£2.99
2. Shooting Star	0 330 32913 8	£2.99
3. On the Wing	0 330 32914 6	£2.99
4. Dream Team	0 330 32915 4	£2.99
GEORGE LAYTON		
The Fib *and other stories*	0 330 35227 X	£3.99

All Macmillan titles can be ordered at your local bookshop or are available by post from:

**Book Service by Post
PO Box 29, Douglas, Isle of Man IM99 1BQ**

Credit cards accepted. For details:
Telephone: 01624 675137
Fax: 01624 670923
E-mail: bookshop@enterprise.net

Free postage and packing in the UK.
Overseas customers: add £1 per book (paperback)
and £3 per book (hardback).